Praise for Edna O'Brien

'For those who first enjoyed *The Country Girls*, this is vintage Edna O'Brien that will engulf them in the familiar world that they cherish'   *Spectator*

'An impressive book: sinewy, spare, clotted with emotion and written in a well-balanced mixture of clipped, elliptical dialogue and rich description ... Violence, hatred and conflict power the story along with great urgency, which makes this a book best read at a single sitting'   *Mail on Sunday*

'A gripping love story which will keep the reader guessing to the end and delight Edna O'Brien's many fans'   *Literary Review*

'This is a fine study of primitive passions, of marginal lives frozen in time ... Edna remains the undisputed literary mistress of her territory. She has a perfect pitch for rural dialogue – the emotional inarticulacy, the spiteful humour'   *Sunday Express*

'You'll turn the pages of this book with the greatest reluctance, and that is because each page is so seductive, so dazzling, you won't want to leave it. Whether the setting is Brooklyn or London or the County Clare itself, richness of detail and atmosphere draws you in. And what novelist in the world can match Edna O'Brien when she explores the human heart? None, I say'   Frank McCourt

In more than twenty books, Edna O'Brien has charted the emotional and psychic landscape of her native Ireland. Often criticized in her own country for her outspoken stance, she has forged a universal audience. Awards and prizes for her work include the Irish PEN Lifetime Achievement Award, Writers' Guild of Great Britain, the Italian Premier Cavour, American National Arts Gold Medal and Ulysses Medal 2006. She grew up in Ireland and now lives in London.

By Edna O'Brien

Edna O'Brien

The Country Girls

PHOENIX

A PHOENIX PAPERBACK

First published in Great Britain in 1960
by Hutchinson
This paperback edition published in 2007
by Phoenix,
an imprint of Orion Books Ltd,
Orion House, 5 Upper St Martin's Lane,
London WC2H 9EA

An Hachette UK company

A CIP catalogue record for this book
is available from the British Library.

Typeset by Input Data Services Ltd, Frome

Printed and bound in Great Britain by
Clays Ltd, St Ives plc

The Orion Publishing Group's policy is to use papers that
are natural, renewable and recyclable products and
made from wood grown in sustainable forests. The logging
and manufacturing processes are expected to conform to
the environmental regulations of the country of origin.

www.orionbooks.co.uk

To my mother

1

I wakened quickly and sat up in bed abruptly. It is only when I am anxious that I waken easily and for a minute I did not know why my heart was beating faster than usual. Then I remembered. The old reason. He had not come home.

Getting out, I rested for a moment on the edge of the bed, smoothing the green satin bedspread with my hand. We had forgotten to fold it the previous night, Mama and me. Slowly I slid on to the floor and the linoleum was cold on the soles of my feet. My toes curled up instinctively. I owned slippers but Mama made me save them for when I was visiting my aunts and cousins; and we had rugs but they were rolled up and kept in drawers until visitors came in the summer-time from Dublin.

I put on my ankle socks.

There was a smell of frying bacon from the kitchen, but it didn't cheer me.

Then I went over to let up the blind. It shot up suddenly and the cord got twisted round it. It was lucky that Mama had gone downstairs, as she was always lecturing me on how to let up blinds properly, gently.

The sun was not yet up, and the lawn was speckled with daisies that were fast asleep. There was dew everywhere.

The grass below my window, the hedge around it, the rusty paling wire beyond that, and the big outer field were each touched with a delicate, wandering mist. And the leaves and the trees were bathed in the mist, and the trees looked unreal, like trees in a dream. Around the forget-me-nots that sprouted out of the side of the hedge were haloes of water. Water that glistened like silver. It was quiet, it was perfectly still. There was smoke rising from the blue mountain in the distance. It would be a hot day.

Seeing me at the window, Bull's-Eye came out from under the hedge, shook himself free of water, and looked up lazily, sadly, at me. He was our sheep-dog and I named him Bull's-Eye because his eyes were speckled black and white, like canned sweets. He usually slept in the turf-house, but last night he had stayed in the rabbit-hole under the hedge. He always slept there to be on the watch-out when Dada was away. I need not ask, my father had not come home.

Just then Hickey called from downstairs. I was lifting my nightdress over my head, so I couldn't hear him at first.

'What? What are you saying?' I asked, coming out on to the landing with the satin bedspread draped around me.

'Good God, I'm hoarse from saying it.' He beamed up at me, and asked, 'Do you want a white or a brown egg for your breakfast?'

'Ask me nicely, Hickey, and call me dotey.'

'Dotey. Ducky. Darling. Honeybunch, do you want a white or a brown egg for your breakfast?'

'A brown one, Hickey.'

'I have a gorgeous little pullet's egg here for you,' he said

2

as he went back to the kitchen. He banged the door. Mama could never train him to close doors gently. He was our workman and I loved him. To prove it, I said so aloud to the Blessed Virgin who was looking at me icily from a gilt frame.

'I love Hickey,' I said. She said nothing. It surprised me that she didn't talk more often. Once she had spoken to me and what she said was very private. It happened when I got out of bed in the middle of the night to say an aspiration. I got out of bed six or seven times every night as an act of penance. I was afraid of hell.

'Yes, I love Hickey,' I thought; but of course what I really meant was that I was fond of him. When I was seven or eight I used to say that I would marry him. I told everyone, including the catechism examiner, that we were going to live in the chicken-run and that we would get free eggs, free milk, and vegetables from Mama. Cabbage was the only vegetable they planted. But now I talked less of marriage. For one thing he never washed himself, except to splash rainwater on his face when he stooped-in over the barrel in the evenings. His teeth were green, and last thing at night he did his water in a peach-tin that he kept under his bed. Mama scolded him. She used to lie awake at night waiting for him to come home, waiting to hear him raise the window while he emptied the peach-tin contents on to the flag outside.

'He'll kill those shrubs under that window, sure as God,' she used to say, and some nights when she was very angry she came downstairs in her nightdress and knocked on his door and asked him why didn't he do that sort of thing outside. But Hickey never answered her, he was too cunning.

3

I dressed quickly, and when I bent down to get my shoes I saw fluff and dust and loose feathers under the bed. I was too miserable to mop the room, so I pulled the covers up on my bed and came out quickly.

The landing was dark as usual. An ugly stained-glass window gave it a mournful look as if someone had just died in the house.

'This egg will be like a bullet,' Hickey called.

'I'm coming,' I said. I had to wash myself. The bathroom was cold, no one ever used it. An abandoned bathroom with a rust stain on the handbasin just under the cold tap, a perfectly new bar of pink soap, and a stiff white face-cloth that looked as if it had been hanging in the frost all night.

I decided not to bother, so I just filled a bucket of water for the lavatory. The lavatory did not flush, and we were expecting a man for months to come and fix it. I was ashamed when Baba my school-friend went up there and said fatally, 'Still out of order?' In our house things were either broken or not used at all. Mama had a new clippers and several new coils of rope in a wardrobe upstairs; she said they'd only get broken or stolen if she brought them down.

My father's room was directly opposite the bathroom. His old clothes were thrown across a chair. He wasn't in there, but I could hear his knees cracking. His knees always cracked when he got in and out of bed. Hickey called me once more.

Mama was sitting by the range, eating a piece of dry bread. Her blue eyes were small and sore. She hadn't slept. She was staring directly ahead at something only she could see, at fate and at the future. Hickey winked at me. He was eating three fried eggs and several slices of home-cured bacon. He dipped his bread into the runny egg yolk and then sucked it.

'Did you sleep?' I asked Mama.

'No. You had a sweet in your mouth and I was afraid you'd choke if you swallowed it whole, so I stayed awake just in case.' We always kept sweets and bars of chocolate under the pillow and I had taken a fruit-drop just before I fell asleep. Poor Mama, she was always a worrier. I suppose she lay there thinking of him, waiting for the sound of a motor-car to stop down the road, waiting for the sound of his feet coming through the wet grass, and for the noise of the gate hasp – waiting, and coughing. She always coughed when she lay down; so she kept old rags that served as hand-kerchiefs in a velvet purse that was tied to one of the posts of the brass bed.

Hickey topped my egg. It had gone hard, so he put little knobs of butter in to moisten it. It was a pullet's egg, that came just over the rim of the big china egg-cup. It looked silly, the little egg in the big cup, but it tasted very well. The tea was cold.

'Can I bring Miss Moriarty lilac?' I asked Mama. I was ashamed of myself for taking advantage of her wretchedness to bring the teacher flowers, but I wanted very much to outdo Baba and become Miss Moriarty's pet.

'Yes, darling, bring anything you want,' Mama said absently. I went over and put my arms round her neck and kissed her. She was the best Mama in the world. I told her so, and she held me very close for a minute as if she would never let me go. I was everything in the world to her, everything.

'Old mammypalaver,' Hickey said. I loosened my fingers that had been locked on the nape of her soft white neck and

I drew away from her, shyly. Her mind was far away, and the hens were not yet fed. Some of them had come down from the yard and were picking Bull's-Eye's food-plate outside the back door. I could hear Bull's-Eye chasing them and the flap of their wings as they flew off cackling violently.

'There's a play in the town hall, missus. You ought to go over,' Hickey said.

'I ought.' Her voice was a little sarcastic. Although she relied on Hickey for everything, she was sharp with him sometimes. She was thinking. Thinking where was he? Would he come home in an ambulance, or a hackney car, hired in Belfast three days ago and not paid for? Would he stumble up the stone steps at the back door waving a bottle of whiskey? Would he shout, struggle, kill her, or apologize? Would he fall in the hall door with some drunken fool and say: 'Mother, meet my best friend Harry. I've just given him the thirteen-acre meadow for the loveliest greyhound ...' All this had happened to us so many times that it was foolish to expect that my father might come home sober. He had gone, three days before, with sixty pounds in his pocket to pay the rates.

'Salt, sweetheart,' said Hickey, putting a pinch between his thumb and finger and sprinkling it on to my egg.

'No, Hickey, don't.' I was doing without salt at that time. As an affectation. I thought it was very grown-up not to use salt or sugar.

'What will I do, Mam?' Hickey asked and took advantage of her listlessness to butter his bread generously on both sides. Not that Mama was stingy with food, but Hickey was getting so fat that he couldn't do his work.

'Go to the bog, I suppose,' she said. 'The turf is ready for footing and we mightn't get a fine day again.'

'Maybe he shouldn't go so far away,' I said. I liked Hickey to be around when Dada came home.

'He mightn't come for a month,' she said. Her sighs would break your heart. Hickey took his cap off the window ledge and went off to let out the cows.

'I must feed the hens,' Mama said, and she took a pot of meal out of the lower oven, where it had been simmering all night.

She was pounding the hens' food outside in the dairy and I got my lunch ready for school. I shook my bottle of cod-liver oil and Parrish's food, so that she'd think I had taken it. Then I put it back on the dresser beside the row of Doulton plates. They were a wedding present, but we never used them in case they'd get broken. There were bills stuffed in behind them. Hundreds of bills. Bills never worried Dada, he just put them behind plates and forgot.

I came out to get the lilac. Standing on the stone step to look across the fields I felt, as I always did, that rush of freedom and pleasure when I looked at all the various trees and the outer stone buildings set far away from the house, and at the fields very green and very peaceful. Outside the paling wire was a walnut tree, and under its shade there were bluebells, tall and intensely blue, a grotto of heaven-blue flowers among the limestone boulders. And my swing was swaying in the wind, and all the leaves on all the tree-tops were stirring lightly.

'Get yourself a little piece of cake and biscuits for your lunch,' Mama said. Mama spoilt me, always giving me little dainties. She was mashing a bucket of meal and potatoes, her head was lowered and she was crying into the hen-food.

'Ah, that's life, some work and others spend,' she said as she went off towards the yard with the bucket. Some of the

7

hens were perched on the rim of the bucket, picking. Her right shoulder sloped more than her left from carrying buckets. She was dragged down from heavy work, working to keep the place going, and at night-time making lamp-shades and fire-screens to make the house prettier.

A covey of wild geese flew overhead, screaming as they passed over the house and down past the elm grove. The elm grove was where the cows went to be cool in summer-time and where the flies followed them. I often played shop there with pieces of broken china and cardboard boxes. Baba and I sat there and shared secrets, and once we took off our knickers in there and tickled one another. The greatest secret of all. Baba used to say she would tell and every time she said that, I gave her a silk hankie or a new tartan ribbon or something.

'Stop moping, my dear little honeybunch,' Hickey said as he got four buckets of milk ready for the calves.

'What do you think of, Hickey, when you're thinking?'

'Dolls. Nice purty little wife. Thinking is a pure cod,' he said. The calves were bawling at the gate and when he went to them each calf nuzzled its head into the bucket and drank greedily. The whitehead with the huge violet eyes drank fastest, so that she could put her nose into the bucket beside her.

'She'll get indigestion,' I remarked.

'Poor creature, 'tis a meat supper she ought to get.'

'I'm going to be a nun when I grow up; that's what I was thinking.'

'A nun you are in my eye. The Kerry Order – two heads on the one pillow.' I felt a little disgusted and went round to pick the lilac. The cement flag at the side of the house was green and slippy. It was where the rain barrel sometimes overflowed and it was just under the window where Hickey emptied the contents of his peach-tin every night.

My sandals got wet when I went over on to the grass.

'Pick your steps,' Mama called, coming down from the yard with the empty bucket in one hand and some eggs in the other hand. Mama knew things before you told her.

The lilac was wet. Drops of water like over-ripe currants fell on to the grass as I broke off each branch. I came back carrying a foam of it like lumber in my arms.

'Don't, it's unlucky,' she called, so I didn't go into the house.

She brought out a piece of newspaper and wrapped it round the steams to keep my dress from getting wet. She brought out my coat and gloves and hat.

''Tis warm, I don't need them,' I said. But she insisted, gently, reminding me again that I had a bad chest. So I put on my coat and hat, got my school-bag, a piece of cake, and a lemonade-bottle of milk for my lunch.

In fear and trembling I set off for school. I might meet him on the way or else he might come home and kill Mama.

'Will you come to meet me?' I asked her.

'Yes, darling; soon as I tidy up after Hickey's dinner, I'll go over the road to meet you.'

'For sure?' I said. There were tears in my eyes. I was always afraid that my mother would die while I was at school.

'Don't cry, love. Come on now, you better go. You have a nice little piece of cake for your lunch and I'll meet you.' She straightened the cap on my head and kissed me three or four times. She stood on the flag to look after me. She was waving. In her brown dress she looked sad, the farther I went the sadder she looked. Like a sparrow in the snow, brown and anxious and lonesome. It was hard to think that she got married one sunny morning in a lace dress and a floppy buttercup hat, and that her eyes were moist with pleasure when now they were watery with tears.

Hickey was driving the cows over to the far field, and I called out to him. He was walking in front of me, his trousers legs tucked into his thick wool socks, his cap turned round so that the peak was on the back of his head. He walked like a clown. I would know his walk anywhere.

'What bird is that?' I asked. There was a bird on the flowering horse-chestnut tree which seemed to be saying:

'Listen here. Listen here.'

'A blackbird,' he replied.

'It's not a black bird. I can see it's a brown bird.'

'All right, smartie. It's a brown bird. I have work to do, I don't go around asking birds their names, ages, hobbies, taste in snails, and so forth. Like these eejits who come over to Burren to look at flowers. Flowers no less. I'm a working man. I carry this place on my shoulders.' It was true that Hickey did most of the work, but even at that the place was going to ruin, the whole 400 acres of it.

'Be off, you chit, or I'll give you a smack on your bottom.'

'How dare you, Hickey.' I was fourteen and I didn't think he should make so free with me.

'Givvus a birdie,' he said, beaming at me with his soft, grey, very large eyes. I ran off, shrugging my shoulders. A birdie was his private name for a kiss. I hadn't kissed him for two years, not since the day Mama gave me the fudge and dared me to kiss him ten times. Dada was in hospital that day recovering from one of his drinking sprees and it was one of the few times I saw Mama happy. It was only for the few weeks immediately after his drinking that she could relax, before it was time to worry again about the next bout. She was sitting on the step of the back door, and I was holding a skein of thread while she wound it into a ball. Hickey came home from the fair and told her the price he got for a heifer and then she dared me to kiss him ten times for the piece of fudge.

I came down the lawn hurriedly, terrified that Dada would appear any minute.

They called it a lawn because it had been a lawn in the old days when the big house was standing; but the Tans burnt the big house and my father, unlike his forbears, had no pride in land and gradually the place went to ruin.

I crossed over the briary part at the lower end of the field. It led towards the wicker gate.

It was crowded with briars and young ferns and stalks of ragwort, and needle-sharp thistles. Under these the ground was speckled with millions of little wild-flowers. Little drizzles of blue and white and violet – little white songs spilling out of the earth. How secret and beautiful and precious they were, hidden in there under the thorns and the young ferns.

I changed the lilac from one arm to the other and came out on to the road. Jack Holland was waiting for me. I got a start when I saw him against the wall. At first I thought it was Dada. They were about the same height and they both wore hats instead of caps.

'Ah, Caithleen, my child,' he greeted me and held the gate while I edged out sideways. The gate only opened back a little and one had to squeeze one's way out. He put the wire catch on and crossed over to the towpath with me.

'How are things, Caithleen? Mother well? Your dad is

conspicuous by his absence. I see Hickey at the creamery these mornings.' I told him things were well, remembering Mama's maxim 'Weep and you weep alone'.

2

'I shall convey you, Caithleen, over the wet winding roads.'

'It's not wet, Jack, and for God's sake don't talk of rain; it's as fatal as opening umbrellas in the house. It just reminds it to rain.'

He smiled and touched my elbow with his hand. 'Caithleen, you must know that poem of Colum's – "wet winding roads, brown bogs and black water, amid my thoughts on white ships and the King of Spain's daughter". Except of course,' said he, grinning to himself, 'my thoughts are nearer home.'

We were passing Mr Gentleman's gate and the padlock was on it.

'Is Mr Gentleman away?' I asked.

'Indubitably. Odd fish, Caithleen. Odd fish.' I said that I didn't think so. Mr Gentleman was a beautiful man who lived in the white house on the hill. It had turret windows and an oak door that was like a church door and Mr Gentleman played chess in the evenings. He worked as a solicitor in Dublin, but he came home at the week-ends and in the summer-time he sailed a boat on the Shannon. Mr Gentleman was not his real name, of course, but everyone called him that. He was French, and his real name was Mr de Maurier, but no one could pronounce it properly, and anyhow he was such a distinguished man with his grey hair and his satin waistcoats that the local people christened him Mr Gentleman. He seemed to like the name very well, and signed his letters J. W. Gentleman. J. W. were the initials of his Christian names and they stood for Jacques and something else.

I remembered the day I went up to his house. It was only a few weeks before that Dada had sent me with a note – it was to borrow money, I think. Just at the top of the tarmac avenue, two red setters shot round the side of the house and jumped on me. I screamed and Mr Gentleman came out the conservatory door and smiled. He led the dogs away and locked them in the garage.

He brought me into the front hall and smiled again. He had a sad face, but his smile was beautiful, remote; and very condescending. There was a trout in a glass case that rested on the hall table and it had a printed sign which read: *Caught by J. W. Gentleman at Lough Derg. Summer 1953. Weight 20 lb.*

From the kitchen came the smell and sizzle of a roast. Mrs Gentleman, who was reputed to be a marvellous cook, must have been basting the dinner.

He opened Dada's envelope with a paper-knife and frowned while he was reading it.

'Tell him that I will look the matter over,' Mr Gentleman said to me. He spoke as if there was a damson stone in his throat. He never lost his French accent, but Jack Holland said this was an affectation.

'Have an orange?' he said, taking two out of the cut-glass bowl on the dining-room table. He smiled and saw me to the door. There was a certain slyness about his smile, and as he shook my hand I had an odd sensation, as if someone were tickling my stomach from the inside. I crossed over the smooth lawn, under the cherry trees, and out on to the tarmac path. He stayed in the doorway. When I looked back the sun was shining on him and on the white Snowcemmed house; and the upstairs windows were all on fire. He waved when I was closing the gate and then went inside. To drink elegant glasses of sherry; to play chess, to eat soufflés and roast venison, I thought, and I was just on the point of thinking about tall eccentric Mrs Gentleman when Jack Holland asked me another question.

'You know something, Caithleen?'

'What, Jack?'

At least he would protect me if we met my father.

'You know many Irish people are royalty and unaware of it. There are kings and queens walking the roads of Ireland, riding bicycles, imbibing tea, ploughing the humble earth, totally unaware of their great heredity. Your mother, now, has the ways and the walk of a queen.'

I sighed. Jack's infatuation with the English language bored me.

He went on: 'My thoughts on white ships and the King of Spain's daughter – except that my thoughts are much nearer home.' He smiled happily to himself. He was composing a paragraph for his column in the local paper – 'Walking in the crystal clear morning with a juvenile lady friend, exchanging snatches of Goldsmith and Colum, the thought flashed my mind that I was moving amidst ...'

The towpath petered out just there and we went on to the road. It was dry and dusty where we walked and we met the carts going over to the creamery and the milk tanks rattled and the owners beat their donkeys with the reins and said, 'Gee-up-there.' Passing Baba's house I walked faster. Her new pink witch bicycle was gleaming against the side wall of their house. Their house was like a doll's house on the outside, pebble-dashed, with two bow windows downstairs and circular flower beds in the front garden. Baba was the veterinary surgeon's daughter. Coy, pretty, malicious Baba was my friend and the person whom I feared most after my father.

'Your mam at home?' Jack finally asked. He hummed some tune to himself.

He tried to sound casual, but I knew perfectly well that this was why he had waited for me under the ivy wall. He had brought over his cow to the paddock he hired from one of our neighbours and then he had waited for me at the wicker gate. He didn't dare come up. Not since the night Dada ordered him out of the kitchen. They were playing cards and Jack had his hand on Mama's knee under the table. Mama didn't protest, because Jack was decent to her, with presents of candied peel and chocolate and samples of jam that he got from commercial travellers. Then Dada let a card fall and bent down to get it; and next thing the table was turned over sideways and the china lamp got broken. My father shouted and pulled up his sleeves, and Mama told me to go to bed. The shouting, high and fierce, came up through the ceiling because my room was directly over the kitchen. Such shouting! It was rough and crushing. Like the noise of a steam-roller. Mama cried and pleaded, and her cry was hopeless and plaintive.

'There's trouble brewing,' said Jack, bringing me from one world of it more abruptly to another. He spoke as if it were the end of the world for me.

We were walking in the middle of the road and from behind came the impudent ring of a bicycle bell. It was Baba, looking glorious on her new puce bicycle. She passed with her head in the air and one hand in her pocket. Her black hair was plaited that day and tied at the tips with blue ribbons that matched her ankle socks exactly. I noticed with envy that her legs were delicately tanned.

She passed us and then slowed down, dragging her left toe along the blue-tarred road, and when we caught up with her she grabbed the lilac out of my arms and said, 'I'll carry that for you.' She laid it into the basket on the front of her bicycle and rode off singing 'I will and I must get married' out loud to herself. So she would give Miss Moriarty the lilac and get all the praise for bringing it.

'You don't deserve this, Caithleen,' he said.

'No, Jack. She shouldn't have taken it. She's a bully.' But he meant something quite different, something to do with my father and with our farm.

We passed the Greyhound Hotel, where Mrs O'Shea was polishing the knocker. She had a hair-net on and pipe-cleaners so tight in her head that you could see her scalp. Her bedroom slippers looked as if the greyhounds had chewed them. More than likely they had. The hotel was occupied chiefly by greyhounds. Mr O'Shea thought he would get rich that way. He went to the dogs in Limerick every night and Mrs O'Shea drank port wine up at the dressmaker's. The dressmaker was a gossip.

'Good morning, Jack; good morning, Caithleen,' she said over-affably. Jack replied coldly; her business interfered with his. He had a grocery and bar up the street, but Mrs O'Shea got a lot of drinkers at night because she kept good fires. The men drank there after hours and she had bribed the guards not to raid her. I almost walked over two hounds that were asleep on the mat outside the shop door. Their noses, black and moist, were jutting out on the pavement.

'Hello,' I said. My mother warned me not to be too free with her as she had given my father so much credit that ten of their cows were grazing on our land for life.

We passed the hotel, the grey, damp ruin that it was; with window-frames rotting and doors scratched all over from the claws of young and nervous greyhounds.

'Did I tell you, Caithleen, that her ladyship has never given a commercial traveller anything, other than fried egg or tinned salmon for lunch?'

'Yes, Jack, you told me.' He had told me fifty times, it was one of his ways of ridiculing her; and by lowering her he hoped to lower the name of the hotel. But the locals liked it, because it was friendly drinking in the kitchen late at night.

We stood for a minute to look over the bridge, at the black-green water that flowed by the window of the hotel basement. It was green water and the willows along the bank made it more green. I was looking to see if there were any fish, because Hickey liked to do a bit of fishing in the evenings, while I waited for Jack to stop hedging and finally tell me whatever it was that he wanted to say.

The bus passed and scattered dust on either side. Something had leaped down below; it might have been a fish. I didn't see it, I was waving to the bus. I always waved. Circles of water were running into one another and when the last circle had dissolved he said, 'Your place is mortgaged; the bank owns it.'

But, like the dark water underneath, his words did not disturb me. They had nothing to do with me; neither the words nor the water; or so I thought as I said good-bye to him and climbed the hill towards the school. 'Mortgage,' I thought, 'now what does that mean?' and puzzling it over I decided to ask Miss Moriarty or better still to look it up in the big black dictionary. It was kept in the school press.

The classroom was in a muddle. Miss Moriarty was bent over a book and Baba was arranging the lilac (my lilac) on the little May altar at the top of the classroom. The smaller children were sitting on the floor mixing all the separate colours of plasticine together; and the big girls were chatting in groups of three or four.

Delia Sheehy was taking cobwebs out of the corners of the ceiling. She had a cloth tied to the end of the window pole and as she moved from one corner to another she dragged the pole along the whitewashed walls and the dusty, faded grey maps. Maps of Ireland and Europe and America. Delia was a poor girl who lived in a cottage with her grandmother. She got all the dirty jobs at school. In winter she lit the fire and cleaned the ashes every morning before the rest of us came in; and every Friday she cleaned the closets with a yard brush and a bucket of Jeyes Fluid water. She had two summer dresses and she washed one every second evening, so that she was always clean and neat and scrubbed looking. She told me that she would be a nun when she grew up.

'You're late, you're going to be killed, murdered, slaughtered,' Baba said to me as I came in. So I went over to apologize to Miss Moriarty.

'What? What's this?' she asked impatiently, as she lifted her head from her book. It was an Italian book. She learnt Italian by post and went to Rome in the summertime. She had seen the Pope and she was a very clever woman. She told me to go to my seat; she was annoyed that I had found her reading an Italian book. On my way down Delia Sheehy whispered to me, 'She never missed you.'

So Baba had sent me to apologize for nothing. I could have gone to my desk unnoticed. I took out an English book and read Thoreau's 'A Winter Walk' – 'Silently we unlatch the door, letting the drift fall in, and step abroad to face the cutting air. Already the stars have lost some of their sparkle, and a dull leaden mist skirts the horizon' – and I was just there when Miss Moriarty called for silence.

'We have great news today,' she said and she was looking at me. Her eyes were small and blue and piercing. You would think she was cross but it was just that she had bad sight from over-reading.

'Our school is honoured,' she said and I felt myself beginning to blush.

'You, Caithleen,' she said, looking directly at me, 'have won a scholarship.' I stood up and thanked her and all the girls clapped. She said that we wouldn't do much work that day as a celebration.

'Where will she be going?' Baba asked. She had put all the lilac in jam-jars and placed them in a dreary half-circle around the statue of the Blessed Virgin. The teacher said the name of the convent. It was at the other end of the county and there was no bus to it.

Delia Sheehy asked me to write in her autograph album and I wrote something soppy. Then a little fold of paper was thrown up from behind, on to my desk. I opened it. It was from Baba. It read:

I'm going there too in September. My father has it all fixed. I have my uniform got. Of course we're paying. It's nicer when you pay. You're a right-looking eejit.

Baba

My heart sank. I knew at once that I'd be getting a lift in their car and that Baba would tell everyone in the convent about my father. I wanted to cry.

The day passed slowly. I was wondering about Mama. She'd be pleased to hear about the scholarship. My education worried her. At three o'clock we were let out; and though I didn't know it, that was my last day at school. I would never again sit in my desk and smell that smell of chalk and mice and swept dust. I would have cried if I had known, or written my name with the corner of a set-square on my desk.

I forgot about the word 'mortgage'.

3

I was wrapping myself up in the cloakroom when Baba
came out. She said 'Cheerio' to Miss Moriarty. She was
Miss Moriarty's pet, even though she was the school dunce.
She wore a white cardigan like a cloak over her shoulders
so that the sleeves dangled down idly. She was full of herself.

'And what in the hell do you want a bloody coat and hat
and scarf for? It's the month of May. You're like a bloody
Eskimo.'

'What's a bloody Eskimo?'

'Mind your own business.' She didn't know.

She stood in front of me, peering at my skin as if it were
full of blackheads or spots. I could smell her soap. It was a
wonderful smell, half perfume, half disinfectant.

'What soap is that you're using?' I asked.

'Mind your own bloody business and use carbolic.
Anyhow, you're a country mope and you don't even wash
in the bathroom, for God's sake. Bowls of water in the
scullery and a face-cloth that your mother made out of an
old rag. What do you use the bathroom for, anyhow?' she
said.

'We have a guest-room,' I said, getting hysterical with
temper.

'Jesus ye have, and there's oats in it. The place is like a

bloody barn with chickens in a box in the window; did ye fix the lavatory chain yet?'

It was surprising that she could talk so fast and yet she wasn't able to write a composition, but bullied me to do it for her.

'Where is your bicycle?' I asked, jealously, as we came out the door. She had cut such a dash with her new bicycle early in the morning that I didn't want to be with her, while she cycled slowly and I walked in a half-run alongside her.

'Left it at home at lunch-time. The wireless said there'd be rain. Flow's your upstairs model?' She was referring to an old-fashioned bicycle of Mama's that I sometimes used.

The two of us went down the towpath towards the village. I could smell her soap. The soap and the neat bands of sticking-plaster, and the cute, cute smile; and the face dimpled and soft and just the right plumpness – for these things I could have killed her. The sticking-plaster was an affectation. It drew attention to her round, soft knees. She didn't kneel as much as the rest of us, because she was the best singer in the choir and no one seemed to mind if she sat on the piano-stool all through Mass and fiddled with the half-moons of her nails: except during the Consecration. She wore narrow bands of sticking-plaster across her knees. She got it for nothing from her father's surgery and people were always asking her if her knees were cut. Grown-ups liked Baba and gave her a lot of attention.

'Any news?' she said suddenly. When she said this I always felt obliged to entertain her, even if I had to tell lies.

'We got a candlewick bedspread from America,' I said and regretted it at once. Baba could boast and when she did everybody listened, but when I boasted everybody laughed and nudged; that was since the day I told them we used our drawing-room for drawing. Not a day passed but Baba said, 'My mammy saw Big Ben on her honeymoon,' and all the girls at school looked at Baba in wonder, as if her mother was the only person ever to have seen Big Ben. Though, indeed, she may have been the only person in our village to have seen it.

Jack Holland rapped his knuckles against the window and beckoned me to come in. Baba followed, and sniffed as soon as we got inside. There was smell of dust and stale porter and old tobacco smoke. We went in behind the counter. Jack took off his rimless spectacles and laid them on an open sack of sugar. He took both my hands in his.

'Your mam is gone a little journey,' he said.

'Gone where?' I asked; with panic in my voice.

'Now, don't be excited. Jack is in charge, so have no fears.'

In charge! Jack had been in charge the night of the concert when the town hall went on fire; jack was in charge of the lorry that De Valera nearly fell through during an election speech. I began to cry.

'Oh, now, now,' Jack said, as he went down to the far end of the shop, where the bottles of wine were. Baba nudged me.

'Go on crying,' she said. She knew we'd get something. He took down a dusty bottle of ciderette and filled two glasses. I didn't see why she should benefit from my miseries.

'To your health,' he said as he handed us the drink. My glass was dirty. It had been washed in portery water and dried with a dirty towel.

'Why do you keep the blind drawn?' Baba said, smiling up at him sweetly.

'It's all a matter of judgement,' he said, seriously, as he put on his glasses.

'These,' he said, pointing to the jars of sweets and the two-pound pots of jam, 'these would suffer from the sunshine.'

The blue blind was faded and was bleached to a dull grey. The cord had come off and the blind was itself torn across the bottom slat, and as he talked to us Jack went over and adjusted it slightly. The shop was cold and sunless and the counter was stained all over with circles of brown.

'Will Mama be long?' I asked, and as soon as I mentioned her name he smiled to himself.

'Hickey could tell you that. If he's not snoring in the hayshed, he could enlighten you,' Jack said. He was jealous of Hickey because Mama relied on Hickey so utterly.

Baba finished her drink and handed him the glass. He sloshed it in a basin of cold water and put it to drain on a metal tray that had 'Guinness is good for you' painted on it. Then he dried his hands most carefully on a filthy, worn, frayed towel; and he winked at me.

'I am going to beg for a favour,' he said to both of us. I knew what it would be.

'What about a kiss each?' he asked. I looked down at a box that was full of white candles.

'Tra ha la la, Mr Holland,' Baba said airily, as she ran out of the shop. I followed her, but unfortunately I tripped over a mouse-trap that he had set inside the door. The trap clicked on my shoe and turned upside down. A piece of fat bacon got stuck to the sole of my shoe.

'These little beastly rodents,' he said, as he took the bacon off my shoe and set the trap again. Hickey said that the shop was full of mice. Hickey said that they tumbled around in the sack of sugar at night, and we bought flour there ourselves that had two dead mice in it. We bought flour in the Protestant shop down the street after that. Mama said that Protestants were cleaner and more honest.

'That little favour,' Jack said earnestly to me.

'I'm too young, Jack,' I said, helplessly; and anyhow I was too sad.

'Touching, most touching. You have a lyrical trend,' he said, as he stroked my pink cheek with his damp hand, and then he held the door as I went out. Just then his mother called him from the kitchen and he ran in to her. I clicked the latch tight, and came out to find Baba waiting.

'Bloody clown, what did you fall over?' She was sitting on an empty porter barrel outside the door, swinging her legs.

'Your dress will get all pink paint from that barrel,' I said.

'It's a pink dress, you eejit. I'm going home with you, I might feck a few rings.' She coveted Mama's rings and was always fitting them on when she came upstairs in our house.

'No, you're not,' I said, firmly. My voice was shaky.

'Yes, I am. I'm going over to get a bunch of flowers. Mammy sent over word at lunch-time to ask your mother could I. Mammy's having tea with the Archbishop tomorrow so we want bluebells for the table.'

'Who's the Archbishop?' I asked, as we had only a Bishop in our diocese.

'Who's the Archbishop! Are you a bloody Protestant or what?' she asked.

I was walking very quickly. I hoped she might get tired of me and go into the paper-shop for a free read of adventure books. The woman in the paper-shop was half blind, and Baba stole a lot of books from there.

I was breathing so nervously that the wings of my nose got wide.

'My nose is getting wider. Will it go back again to normal?' I asked.

'Your nose,' she said, 'is always wide. You've a nose like a bloody petrol-pump.'

We passed the fair-green and the market-house and the rows of tumbling, musty little shops on either side of us. We passed the bank, which was a lovely two-storey house and had a polished knocker; and we crossed the bridge. Even on a still day like that, the noise from the river was urgent and rushing, as if it were in full flood.

Soon we were out of the town and climbing the hill that led to the forge. The hill rose between the trees and it was dark in there because the leaves almost met overhead. And it was quiet except for the clink–clank from the forge where Billy Tuohey was beating a horseshoe into shape. Overhead the birds were singing and fussing and twittering.

'Those bloody birds get on my nerves,' she said, making a face up at them.

Billy Tuohey nodded to us through the open window space. It was so smoky in there we could hardly see him. He lived with his mother in a cottage at the back of the forge. They kept bees and he was the only man around who grew brussels sprouts. He told lies, but they were nice lies. He told us that he sent his photo to Hollywood and got a cable back to say *Come quick you have the biggest eyes since Greta Garbo.* He told us that he dined with the Aga Khan at the Galway races and that 'they played snooker after dinner. He told us that his shoes were stolen when he left them outside the door of the hotel. He told us so many lies and so many stories, his stories filled in the nights, the dark nights, and their colours were exotic like the colours of the turf flames. He danced jigs and reels too and he played the accordion very well.

'What's Billy Tuohey?' she asked suddenly as if she wanted to frighten me.

'A blacksmith,' I said.

'Jesus, you lumping eejit. What else?'

'What?'

'Billy Tuohey is a fly boy.'

'Does he get girls into trouble?' I asked.

'No. He keeps bees,' she said and sighed. I was a dull dog.

We came to her gate and she ran in with her schoolbag. I didn't wait for her; I didn't want her to come. The wild bees from a nest in the stone wall made a sleepy, murmuring sound, and the fruit trees outside the barber's house were shedding the last of their petals. There was a pool of white and pink petals under the apple tree, and the children stepped over the petals, crushing them under their bare feet. The two youngest were hanging over the wall saying 'good afternoona' to everyone who went by. They were eating slices of bread-and-jam.

'What do Mickey the Barber's eat for breakfast?' she asked as she caught up with me. The barber's children were always known as Mickey the Barber's because their father's name was Mickey and there were too many children for one to remember their separate names.

'Bread and tea, I suppose.'

'Hair soup, you fool. What do Mickey the Barber's eat for lunch?'

'Hair soup.' I felt very smart now.

'No. Jugged hair, you eejit.' She picked a stalk of tough grass off the side of the ditch, chewed it thoughtfully, and spat it out. She was bored and I didn't know why she came at all.

As we came near our gate I ran on ahead of her and almost walked over him. He was sitting on the ground with his back against the bark of an elm tree and there were shadows of leaves on his face. The shadows moved. He was asleep.

I went over and shook him. 'Hickey, Hickey.'

He blinked for a few seconds, then opened his grey eyes and looked at me with a sleepy, stupid stare. He had been dreaming.

'What's happened? Where's Mama? Is he at home?' the questions flew out of me.

'For God's sake take it easy,' he said; and yet he had put an arm round me and was comforting my cheek with his hand.

'Where's Mama?' I asked again.

'She's gone to Tintrim,' he said.

Tintrim was her old home. Her father and her unmarried sister lived there. It was a small, whitewashed house with ivy on the walls, and it was situated on a rocky island in the great lake of the Shannon. It was about three miles from the mainland. Another farmer lived there too, and both families shared the one boat. They came across on Fridays for messages and for Grandfather's old age pension; and of course they came on Sundays to Mass. After Mass they bought papers and got a cup of tea from the woman in the paper-shop, while Grandfather went off to have a pint of stout. He was an old man and there was always a dribble on his white beard. He was too old to row the boat across; but his neighbour, Tom O'Brien, was a young man, and very amiable. Tom rowed, while Grandfather raved about the old days and the time when the Shannon was frozen for three months; and he had stories to tell about the young men who hid in his hayloft from the Black-and-Tans. Always the same stories, but Tom O'Brien and his family listened to Grandfather as if they had never heard these stories before. Mrs O'Brien and my Aunt Molly had great trouble keeping on their hats because even on a summer's day there was a high wind, and sometimes a Storm would blow up all of a sudden and the waves would splash in over the edge of the boat. It was an old boat, painted green.

So Mama was gone there, even though she didn't like it. She said the ivy kept out the light from the kitchen and she could never sleep there because the sound of water worried her. She dreaded water. It was Friday, so probably she would meet Tom O'Brien in the village of Tintrim. I wondered why she had gone at all. It wasn't like her. She had never left me before, never. I thought that perhaps she went to ask Grandfather if herself and myself could live there. I liked the prospect of living there. My Aunt Molly was nice and she read love stories aloud to me at night. They had an old-fashioned wireless that you listened to by putting on earphones; and they had pet bantams that were always in around the house. It was nice there in the summer-time. Fields of corn at the side of the house, and bamboo trees thick and luxuriant along by the water's edge. There was a sandy beach where Aunt Molly and I sat and read love stories and my grandfather never got drunk. I was thinking of these things, because I dreaded asking Hickey the next question, but in the end I asked, 'Did he come back?'

'He came back to change his shirt,' Hickey said, with sarcasm.

'Did he hit her?'

'Hasn't he always to hit someone when he's drunk? If it's not her 'tis me; and 'tis the dog if it's neither of us.' Just then Baba came in the gate eating a banana.

'You could have waited for me,' she said, glaring at me.

'Hello, Shirley Temple,' Hickey said to her; and to me: 'Your mam said that you were to stay with Baba.'

'No, Hickey, I'll stay at home. You'll mind me.' He shook his head. So he didn't want me. He didn't love me. He wouldn't make the sacrifice and stay in at night. He couldn't do without his porter and Maisie's greasy face. Maisie worked in the bar of the Greyhound Hotel. The zips of her skirts were always burst and she had no teeth, but Hickey liked her. She was fat like him, and jolly.

'Stay with us,' Baba said, throwing her banana skin on a fresh cow-pat and scattering a host of flies in all directions. I looked at Hickey and interceded for help but I could not reach him. No one spoke. I hung my head and saw the flies come back to the cow-pat, and settle on it like burnt raisins on top of a dark cake.

'I couldn't mind you,' he said finally. 'I have to milk cows and feed calves and feed hens. I have to carry this place on my shoulders.' He was enjoying his importance.

'I don't need minding,' I said. 'I just want you to stay in at night with me.' But he shook his head. I knew that I would have to go. So I was determined to be difficult.

'What about my nightdress?' I asked.

'Go up for it,' Baba said calmly. How could they be so calm when my teeth were chattering?

'I can't. I'm afraid.'

'Afraid of what?' asked Hickey. 'Sure, he's in Limerick by now.'

'Are you sure?'

31

'Sure! Didn't he come down and get a lift on the mail-car? You won't see him for ten or eleven days, not till all the money is spent.'

'Come on, Booby, I'll go with you,' Baba said. I wanted to ask Hickey if Mama was all right. I whispered.

'Can't hear you.'

I whispered again.

'Can't hear you.'

I let it go. He went over across the field whistling, and we went up the avenue. The avenue was full of weeds and there were wheel ruts on either side of it from carts that went up and down every day.

'Have you nits?' she asked, making a face.

'I don't know. Why?'

'If you had nits, you couldn't stay. Couldn't have things crawling over my pillow; creepy-crawly things like that would carry you off.'

'Off where?'

'To the Shannon.'

'That's daft.'

'No. You're daft,' she said, lifting up a coil of my hair and looking carefully at the scalp. Then suddenly she dropped the coil of hair as if she had seen some terrible disease. 'Have to dose you. You're full of bugs and fleas and flits and flies and all sorts of vermin.' I came out in gooseflesh.

Bull's-Eye was eating bread off an enamel plate that someone had put on the flag for him. Poor Bull's-Eye, so someone had remembered.

Inside, the kitchen was untidy and the range was out. Mama's wellingtons were in the middle of the floor and there were two cans of milk on the kitchen table; so was the stationery box. It was in it she kept her powder and lipstick and things. Her powder-puff was gone and her rosary beads were taken from the nail off the dresser. She was gone. Really gone.

'Come upstairs with me,' I said to Baba. My knees were shaking uncontrollably.

'Anything a person could eat?' she asked, opening the breakfast-room door. She knew that Mama kept tins of biscuits in there behind one of the curtains. The room was dark and sad and dusty. The what-not, with its collection of knick-knacks and chocolate-box lids and statues and artificial flowers, looked silly now that Mama wasn't there. The crab shells that she used as ashtrays were all over the room. Baba picked up a couple and put them down again.

'Jesus, this place is like a bloody bazaar,' said Baba, going over to the what-not to salute all the statues.

'Hello, Saint Anthony. Hello Saint Jude, patron of hopeless cases.' She picked up an Infant of Prague and the head came off in her hand. She roared laughing, and when I offered her a biscuit from a tin of assorted ones she took all the chocolate ones and put them in her pocket.

Then she saw the butter on the tiled kerb of the fireplace. Mama kept it there in summer-time to keep it cool. She picked up a couple of pounds. 'Might as well have this towards your keep. We'll go up and have a look at her jewellery,' she said.

Mama had rings that Baba coveted. They were nice rings. Mama got them for presents when she was a young girl. She had been to America. She had a lovely face then. Round, sallow face with the most beautiful, clear, trusting eyes. Turquoise blue. And hair that had two colours. Some strands were red-gold and some were brown, so that it couldn't possibly have been dyed. I had hair like her. But Baba put it out at school that I dyed mine.

'Your hair is like old mattress stuffing,' she said when I told her what I was thinking.

Soon as we went into the guest-room where the rings were, the ewer rattled in the basin, and the flowers that were laid into it moved, as if propelled by a gentle wind. They weren't flowers really but ears of corn that Mama had covered with pieces of silver paper and gold paper. They were displayed with stalks of pampas grass that she had dyed pink. They were garish, like colours in a carnival. But Mama liked them. She was house proud. Always doing something.

'Get out the rings and stop looking into the damn' mirror.' The mirror was clouded over with green spots but I looked in it out of habit. I got out the brown and gold box where the jewellery was kept and Baba fitted on everything. The rings and the two pearl brooches and the amber necklace that came down to her stomach.

'You could give me one of these rings,' she said, 'if you weren't so bloody stingy.'

'They're Mama's, I couldn't,' I said, in a panic.

'They're Mama's, I couldn't,' she said, and my voice was high and thin and watery when she mimicked it. She opened the wardrobe and got out the green georgette dance-dress and then admired herself in the clouded mirror and danced a little on her toes. She was very pretty when she danced. I was clumsy.

'Sssh, I thought I heard something,' I said. I was almost certain that I heard a step downstairs.

'Ah, it's the dog,' she said.

'I better go down, he might knock over one of the cans

of milk. Did we leave the back door open?' I ran down and stopped dead in the kitchen doorway, because there he was. There was my father, drunk, his hat pushed far back on his head and his white raincoat open. His face was red and fierce and angry. I knew that he would have to strike someone.

'A nice thing to come into an empty house. Where's your mother?'

'I don't know.'

'Answer my question.' I dreaded looking at those eyes which were blue and huge and bulging. Like glass eyes.

'I don't know.'

He came over and gave me a punch under the chin so that my two rows of teeth chattered together and with his wild lunatic eyes he stared at me. 'Always avoiding me. Always avoiding your father. You little s——. Where's your mother or I'll kick the pants off you.'

I shouted for Baba and she came tripping down the stairs with a beaded bag of Mama's hanging from her wrist. He took his hands off me at once. He didn't like people to think that he was brutal. He had time name of being a gentleman, a decent man who wouldn't hurt a fly.

'Good evening, Mr Brady,' she said.

'Well, Baba. Are you a good girl?' I was edging nearer the door that led to the scullery. I'd be safer there where I could run. I could smell the whiskey. He had hiccups and every time he hicked Baba laughed. I hoped he wouldn't catch her, or he might kill both of us.

'Mrs Brady is gone away. It's her father, he's not well. Mrs Brady got word to go and Caithleen is to stay with us.' She was eating a chocolate biscuit while she spoke and there were crumbs in the corners of her pretty lips.

'She'll stay and look after me. That's what she'll do.' He spoke very loud and he was shaking his fist in my direction.

'Oh.' Baba smiled. 'Mr Brady, there is someone coming to look after you – Mrs Burke from the cottages. As a matter of fact we have to go down now and let her know that you're here.' He said nothing. He let out another hiccup. Bull's-Eye came in and was brushing my leg with his white hairy tail.

'We better hurry,' Baba said, and she winked at me. He took a pile of notes out of his pocket and gave Baba one folded, dirty pound note.

'Here,' he said, 'that's for her keep. I don't take anything for nothing.' Baba thanked him and said he shouldn't have bothered and we left.

'Jesus, he's blotto, let's run,' she said, but I couldn't run, I was too weak.

'And we forgot the damn' butter,' she added. I looked back and saw him coming out the gate after us, with great purposeful strides.

'Baba,' he called. She asked me if we should run. He called again. I said we'd better not because I wasn't able.

We stood until he caught up with us.

'Give me back that bit of money. I'll settle up with your father myself. I'll be getting him over here next week to do a few jobs.'

He took it and walked off quickly. He was hurrying to the public house or maybe to catch the evening bus to Portumna. He had a friend there who kept racehorses.

'Mean devil, he owes my daddy twenty pounds,' Baba said. I saw Hickey coming over the field and I waved to him. He was driving the cows. They straggled across the field, stopping for a minute, as cows will, to stare idly at nothing. Hickey was whistling and the evening being calm and gentle his song went out across the field. A stranger going the road might have thought that ours was a happy farm; it seemed so, happy and rich and solid in the copper light of the warm evening. It was a red cut-stone house Set among the trees, and in the evening-time, when the sun was going down, it had a lustre of its own, with fields rolling out from it in a flat, uninterrupted expanse of green.

'Hickey, you told me a lie. He came back and nearly killed me.' Hickey was within a few yards from us, standing between two cows with a hand on each of them.

'Why didn't you hide?'

'I walked straight into him.'

'What did he want?'

'To fight as always.'

'Mean devil. He gave me a pound for her keep and took It back again,' Baba said.

'If I had a penny for every pound he owes me,' Hickey said, shaking his head fondly. We owed Hickey a lot of money and I was worried that he might leave us and get a job with the forestry, where he'd be paid regularly.

'Sure you won't go, Hickey?' I pleaded.

'I'll be off to Birmingham when the summer is out,' he said. My two greatest fears in life were that Mama would die of cancer and that Hickey would leave. Four women in the village died of cancer. Baba said it was something to do with not having enough babies. Baba said that all nuns get cancer. Just then I remembered about my scholarship and I told Hickey. He was pleased.

'Oh, you'll be a toff from now on,' he said. The brown cow lifted her tail and wet the grass.

'Anyone want lemonade?' he asked and we ran off. He slapped the cow on the back and she moved lazily. The cows in front moved too, and Hickey followed them with a new whistle. The evening was very still.

4

Baba called her mother – 'Martha, Martha' – as we went into the hall. It was a tiled hall and it smelt of floor polish.

We went up the carpeted stairs. A door opened slowly and Martha put her head out.

'Sssh, sssh,' she said and beckoned us to come in. We went into the bedroom and she shut the door quietly behind us.

'Hello, horror,' Declan said to Baba. He was her younger brother. He was eating a leg of a chicken.

There was a cooked chicken on a plate in the centre of the big bed. It was over-cooked and was falling apart.

'Take off your coat,' Martha said to me. She seemed to be expecting me. Mama must have called. Martha looked pale, but then she was always pale. She had a pale madonna face with eyelids always lowered and behind them her eyes were big and dark so that you could not see their colour, but they reminded one of purple pansies. Velvety. She was wearing red velvet shoes with little crusts of silver on the front of them, and her room smelt of perfume and wine and grown-upness. She was drinking red wine.

'Where's the aul fella?' Baba asked.

'I don't know.' Martha shook her head. Her black hair,

which was usually piled high on her head, hung below her shoulders and curled upwards a little.

'Whatja bring the chicken in here?' Baba asked.

'Whatja think?' Declan said, throwing her the wishbone.

'So's the aul fella won't get it,' she said, addressing the photograph of her father on the mantelshelf. She shot at him with her right hand and said, 'Bang, bang.'

Martha gave me a wing of chicken. I dipped it in the saltcellar and ate it. It was delicious.

'Your mam's gone away for a few days,' she said to me and once again I felt the lump in my throat. Sympathy was bad for me. Not that Martha was motherly. She was too beautiful and cold for that.

Martha was what the villagers called fast. Most nights she went down to the Greyhound Hotel, dressed in a tight black suit with nothing under the jacket only a brassière, and with a chiffon scarf knotted at her throat. Strangers and commercial travellers admired her. Pale face, painted nails, blue-black pile of hair, madonna face, perched on a high stool in the lounge bar of the Greyhound Hotel, they thought she looked sad. But Martha was not ever sad, unless being bored is a form of sadness. She wanted two things from life and she got them – drink and admiration.

'There's trifle in the pantry. Molly left it there,' she said to Baba. Molly was a sixteen-year-old maid, from a small farm up the country. During her first week in Brennans' she wore wellingtons all the time, and when Martha reproved her for this she said that she hadn't anything else. Martha often beat Molly, and locked her in a bedroom whenever Molly asked to go to a dance in the town hall. Molly told the dressmaker that 'they', meaning the Brennans, ate big roasts every day while she herself got sausages and old potato mash. But this may have been just a story. Martha was not mean. She took pride and vengeance in spending his money, but like all drinkers she was reluctant to spend on anything other than drink.

Baba came in with a Pyrex dish that was half full of trifle, and she set it down on the bed along with saucers and dessert-spoons. Her mother dished it out. The pink trifle with a slice of peach, a glacé cherry, a cut banana, and uneven lumps of sponge cake, all reminded mc of the days when we had trifle at home. I could see Mama piling it on our plates, my father's, my own, and Hickey's, and leaving only a spoon- ful for herself in the bottom of the bowl. I could see her getting angry and wrinkling her nose if I protested, and my father snapping at me to shut up; and Hickey sniggering and saying, 'All the more for us.' I was thinking of this when I heard Baba say, 'She doesn't eat trifle,' meaning me. Her mother divided the extra plate between the three of them and my mouth watered while I watched them eat.

'Martha, hey, old Martha, what will I be when I grow up?' Declan asked his mother. He was smoking a cigarette and was learning to inhale.

'Get out of this dive – be something – somebody. An actor, something exciting,' Martha said as she looked in the mirror and squeezed a blackhead out of her chin,

'Were you famous, Mammy?' Baba asked the face in the mirror. The face raised its eyes and sighed, remembering. Martha had been a ballet dancer. But she gave up her career for marriage, or so she had said.

'Why did you chuck in?' Baba asked, knowing the answer well.

'Actually I was too tall,' said Martha, doing a little dance away from the mirror and across the room; waving a red georgette scarf in the air.

'Too tall? Jesus, stick to the same story,' Baba reminded her mother, and her mother went on dancing on the tips of her toes.

'I could have married a hundred men, a hundred men cried at my wedding,' Martha said, and the children began to clap.

'One was an actor, one was a poet, a dozen were in the diplomatic service.' Her voice trailed off as she went over to speak to her two pet goldfish on the dressing-table.

'Diplomatic service – better than this dump,' Baba mourned.

'Christ,' Martha replied, and then a car hooted and they all jumped.

'The chicken, the chicken,' said Martha and she put it in the wardrobe with an old bed-jacket over it. In the wardrobe there were summer dresses and a white fur evening-cape.

'Get out, be doing something in the kitchen – your exercises,' Martha said as she got down her toothbrush and began to wash her teeth over the handbasin. Their house was very modern with handbasins in the two front bed-rooms. Later she followed us down to the kitchen.

'All right?' she asked, breathing close to Baba.

'He'll say you give your damn' teeth great care,' Baba laughed, and then made a straight face when she heard him come in the back door. He was carrying an empty Winchester, an open packet of cotton wool, and a shoe-box full of garden peas.

'Mammy. Declan. Baba.' He saluted each of them. I was behind the door and he couldn't see me. His voice was low and hoarse and slightly sarcastic. Martha knelt down and got his dinner out of the lower oven of the Aga cooker. It was a fried chop that had gone dry and some fried onions that looked very sodden. She put the plate on an elaborately laid silver tray. The Brennans, my mother always claimed, would make a meal on cutlery and doyleys.

'I thought we had chicken today, Mammy,' he said, taking off his glasses and cleaning them with a large white handkerchief.

'That half-wit Molly left the meat-safe open and Rover got off with the chicken,' Martha said calmly.

'Stupid fool. Where is she?'

'Gallivanting,' said Baba.

'Molly will have to be chastised, punished, do you hear me, Mammy?' and Martha said yes and that she wasn't deaf. It was then I coughed, because I wanted him to see me, to know that I was there. He had his back to me, but he turned round quickly.

'Ah, Caithleen, Caithleen, my lovely child.' He came over and put his arms on my shoulders and kissed me lightly on either cheek. He had had a few drinks.

'I wish, Caithleen, that others, others,' he said, waving his hand in the air, 'others would be as clever and gentle as you are.' Baba stuck her tongue out and as if he had eyes in the back of his head he turned round to address her.

'Baba.'

'Yes, Daddy?' She was smiling now, a sweet loganberry smile, and the dimples in her cheeks were just the right hollowness.

'Can you cook peas?'

'No.'

'Can your mother cook peas?'

'I don't know.' Martha had gone into the hall to answer

43

the telephone; and she came back writing a name into an address book.

'They want you to go to Cooriganoir. People by the name of O'Brien. They have a heifer dying. It's urgent,' she said, as she wrote directions on how to find the place into the notebook.

'Can you cook peas, Mammy?'

'They want you to go at once. They said you were late the last time and the horse died and a foal was born lame.'

'Stupid, stupid, stupid,' he said. I didn't know whether he meant his wife, or the family on Cooriganoir. He drank milk from a jug that was on the dresser. He drank it noisily, you could hear it going down the tunnel of his throat.

Martha sighed and lit herself a cigarette. His dinner had gone cold on the tray and he hadn't touched it.

'Better look up how to cook peas, Mammy,' he said. She began to whistle softly, ignoring him, whistling as if she were walking over a dusty mountain road and whistled to keep herself company, or to recall a dog that had followed a rabbit through a hedge and over a field. He went out and banged the door.

'Is he gone?' Declan called from the pantry, where he had locked himself in. His father often asked Declan to go with him, but Declan preferred to sit around smoking and talking to Martha about his career. He wanted to be a film actor.

'Are we going to the play tonight, Martha?' Baba asked.

'With knobs on! He can cook his own bloody peas. Such arrogance. I was eating peas when his thick lump of a mother was feeding them nettle-tops. Jesus.' It was the first time I saw Martha flushed.

'*You* better not come to the play. Your aul fella might be

getting sick and puking all over the damn' floor,' Baba said to me.

'She is coming,' said Declan. 'Isn't she, Martha?'

Martha smiled at me, and said I was, of course.

'Well, if Mr Gentleman is there, I'm sitting next to him,' Baba said, tossing her black plaits with a shake of her head.

'No. You are not. I am,' Martha said, smiling. Martha had dimples too, but they were not so hollow as Baba's and not so pretty, because her skin was very white.

'Anyhow he has some dame in Dublin. A chorus girl,' Baba said, and she lifted up her dress to show her knees, because that was how chorus girls behaved.

'Liar. Liar,' Declaim called her and he threw the box of peas at her. They were scattered all over the floor and I had to get down on my knees to pick them up. Baba opened several pods and ate the delicious young peas. I put the empty pods in the fire. Martha went upstairs to get ready and Declan went into the drawing-room to play the gramophone.

'Who told you about Mr Gentleman?' I asked, timidly.

'You did,' she said, giving me one of her brazen, blue-eyed stares.

'I did not. How dare you?' I was trembling with anger.

'How dare you say how dare you to me – in my own house?' she said, as she went off to bathe her feet before going to the play. She shouted back from the hallway, to ask if my mother still washed hers in a milk-bucket at the end of the kitchen table. And for a second I could see Mama in the lamplight bathing her poor corns, to soften them, before she began paring them with a razor-blade.

The grandfather clock in the hall struck five, and the sky was very dark outside. A wind began to rise, and an old bucket rattled along the gravel path. The rain came quite suddenly, and Baba shouted down to me to bring in the clothes off the line, for Christ's sake. It was a shower of hailstones and they beat against the window like bullets, so that you expected the glass to break. I ran out for the clothes and got wet to the skin. I thought of Mama and I hoped that she was in out of it. There was very little shelter along the road from our village to the village of Tintrim, and Mama was very shy and wouldn't dare ask for a shelter in a house that she passed by. The rain was over in ten minutes and the sun appeared in a rift between the clouds. The apple blossoms were blown all over the grass, and there was a line of water on the branch of the tree that rose outside the kitchen window. I folded the sheets and smelt them for a minute, because there is no smell so pleasant as that of freshly washed linen. Then I put them to dry on the rack over the Aga cooker because they were still a little damp, and after that I went upstairs to Baba's room.

5

We set out for the town hail just before seven. Mr Brennan was not home, so we left the table set and when Martha was upstairs getting ready I put a damp napkin round his plate of sandwiches. I was sorry for Mr Brennan. He worked hard and he had an ulcer.

Declan went on ahead. He thought it was cissyish to walk with girls.

The sun was going down and it made a fire in the western part of the sky. Running out from the fire, there were pathways of colour, not red like the sun, but a warm, flushed pink. The sky above it was a naked blue, and higher still, over our heads, great eiderdowns of clouds sailed serenely by. Heaven was up there. I knew no one in Heaven. Except old women in the village who had died, but no one belonging to me.

'My mammy is the best-looking woman round here,' Baba said. In fact I thought my mother was; with her round, pale, heart-breaking face and her grey, trusting eyes; but I didn't say so because I was staying in their house. Martha did look lovely. The setting sun, or maybe it was the coral necklace, gave her eyes a mysterious orange glow.

'BBBIP BBBIP,' said Hickey as he cycled past us. I was always sorry for Hickey's bicycle. I expected it to collapse under his weight. The tyres looked flat. He was carrying a can of milk on the handlebar and a rush basket with a live hen clucking in it. Probably for Mrs O'Shea in the Greyhound Hotel. Hickey always treated his friends when Mama was away. I supposed Mama had the chickens counted, but Hickey could say the fox came. The foxes were always coming into the yard in broad daylight and carrying off a hen or a turkey.

In front of us, like specks of brown dust, the hordes of midges were humming to themselves under the trees and my ears were itchy after we had passed through that part of the road near the forge, where there was a grove of beech trees.

'Hurry,' said Martha, and I took longer steps. She wanted seats in the front row. Important people sat there. The doctor's wife and Mr Gentleman and the Connor girls. The Connor girls were Protestants but well thought of. They passed us just then in their station-wagon and hooted. It was their way of saying hello. We nodded back to them. There were two alsatians in the back of the car and I was glad they hadn't offered us a lift. I was afraid of alsatians. The Connor girls had a sign on their gate which said 'Beware of Dogs'. They spoke in haughty accents, they rode horses and followed the Hunt in winter-time. When they went to race meetings they had walking-sticks that they could sit on. They never spoke to me, but Martha was invited there for afternoon tea once a year. In the summer-time.

We mounted the great flight of concrete steps and went into the porch that led to the town hall. There was a fat woman in the ticket office and we could see only the top half of her. She was wearing a puce dress that had millions of sequins stitched on to it. There were crusts of mascara on her lashes, and her hair was dyed puce to match her dress. It was fascinating to watch the sequins shining as if they were moving on the bodice of her dress.

'Her bubs are dancing,' Baba said and we both sniggered. We were sniggering as we held the double doors for Martha to enter. Martha liked to make an entrance.

'Children, stop laughing,' she said, as if we didn't belong to her.

An actor with pancake make-up beamed at us and went on ahead to find our seats. Martha had given him three blue tickets.

The country boys in the back of the hall whistled as we came in. It was their habit to stand there and pass remarks about the girls as they came in, and then laugh, or whistle if the girl was pretty. They were in their old clothes but most of them probably had their Sunday shoes on, and there was a strong smell of hair oil.

'Uncouth,' Martha said under her breath. It was her favourite word for most of her husband's customers. There was one nice boy who smiled at me, he had black curly hair and a red, happy face. I knew he was on the hurley team.

We were sitting in the front row. Martha sat next to the eldest Connor girl, Baba next to her, and I was on the outside. Mr Gentleman was farther in, near the younger Connor girl. I saw the back of his neck and the top of his collar before I sat down. I was glad to know that he was there.

The hall was almost dark. Curtains of black cloth had been put over the windows and pinned to the window-frames at the four corners. The light from the six oil-lamps at the front of the stage barely showed people to their seats.

Two of the lamps smoked and the globes were black.

I looked back to see if there was any sign of Hickey. I looked through the rows of chairs, then along the rows of stools behind the chairs, and farther back still I searched with my eyes along the planks that were laid on porter barrels. He was at the end of the last row of planks with Maisie next to him. The cheapest seats. They were laughing. The back of the hall was full of girls laughing. Girls with curly hair, girls with shiny black coils of it, like bunches of elderberries, falling on to their shoulders, girls with moist blackberry eyes; smirking and talking and waiting. Miss Moriarty was two rows behind us and she bowed lightly to acknowledge that she saw me. Jack Holland was writing into a notebook.

A bell gonged and the dusty grey curtain was drawn slowly back. It got stuck half-way. The boys at the back booed. I could see the actor with the pancake make-up pulling a string from the wings of the stage and finally he came out and pushed the curtain back with his hands. The crowd cheered.

On stage were four girls in cerise blouses, black frilly pants, and black hard hats. They had canes under their arms and they tap-danced. I wished that Mama were there. In all the excitement I hadn't thought of her for over an hour. She would have enjoyed it especially when she heard about the scholarship.

The girls danced off, two to the right and two to the left, and then a man carrying a banjo came on and sang sad songs. He could turn his two eyes inwards and when he did everyone laughed.

After that came a laughing sketch where two clowns got in and out of boxes and then the woman in the puce dress sang 'Courting in the Kitchen'. She waved to the audience to join in with her and towards the end they did. She was awful.

'And now, ladies and gentlemen, there will be a short interval, during which time we will sell tickets that will be raffled immediately before the play. And the play, as you probably know, is the one and only, the heart-warming, tear-making *East Lynne*,' said the man with the pancake make-up.

I had no money but Martha bought me four tickets.

'If you win it's mine,' said Baba. Mr Gentleman passed his packet of cigarettes all along the front row. Martha took one and leaned forward to thank him. Baba and I ate Turkish Delight.

When the tickets were sold the actor came down and stood under the oil-lamps; he put the duplicate ones into a big hat and looked around for someone to draw the winning numbers. Children were usually picked to do this, as they were supposed to be honest. He looked down the hall and then he looked at Baba and me and he chose us. We stood up and faced the audience and she picked the first number and I picked the next one. He called out the winning numbers. He called them three times, but nothing happened. You could hear a pin drop. He said them once more and he was just on the point of asking us to draw two more tickets when there came a shout from the back of the hall.

'Here, down here,' people said.

'Now you must come forward and show your tickets.'

People liked winning but they were ashamed to come up and collect the prizes. At last they shuffled out from among the standing crowd and the two winners came hesitantly up the passage. One was an albino and the other was a young boy. They showed their tickets, collected their ten shillings each, and went back in a half-run to the darkness at the end of the hall.

'And how about a little song from our two charming friends here?' he said, putting a hand on each of our shoulders.

'Yes,' said Baba who was always looking for an excuse to show off her clear, light, early-morning voice. She began: 'As I was going one morning, 'twas in the month of May, a mother and her daughter I spied along the way,' and I opened and closed my mouth to pretend that I was singing too. But she stopped all of a sudden and nudged me to carry on, and there I was, seen by everyone in the hall with my mouth wide-open as if I had lockjaw. I blushed and faded back to my seat and Baba went on with her song. 'Witch,' I said, under my breath.

East Lynne began. There was dead silence everywhere, except for voices on the stage.

Then I heard noise in the back of the hall, and shuffling as if someone had fainted. A flashlamp travelled up along the passage and as it came level with us I saw that it was Mr Brennan.

'Jesus, it's about the chicken,' Baba said to her mother, as Mr Brennan called Martha out. He crossed over, stooping so as not to be in the way of the stage and he whispered to Mr Gentleman. Both of them went out. I heard the door being shut noisily and I was glad that they were gone. The play was so good, I didn't want to miss a line.

But the door was opened again and the beam of the flashlamp came up along the hall. A thought struck me that they wanted me and then I put it aside again. But it was me. Mr Brennan tapped me on the shoulder and whispered,

'Caithleen love, I want you a minute.' My shoes creaked as I went down the hall on tip-toe. I expected it was something about my father.

Outside in the porch they were all talking – Martha and the parish priest, and Mr Gentleman and the solicitor and Hickey. Hickey had his back to me and Martha was crying. It was Mr Gentleman who told me.

'Your mother, Caithleen, she's had a little accident'; he spoke slowly and gravely and his voice was unsteady.

'What kind of an accident?' I asked, staring wildly at all the faces. Martha was suffocating into her handkerchief.

'A little accident,' Mr Gentleman said, again, and the parish priest repeated it.

'Where is she?' I asked, quickly, wildly. I wanted to get to her at once. At once. But no one answered.

'Tell me,' I said. My voice was hysterical and then I realized that I was being rude to the parish priest, and I asked again, only more gently.

'Tell her, 'tis better to tell her,' I heard Hickey say behind my back. I turned round to ask him but Mr Brennan shook his head and Hickey blushed under the grey stubble of his two-day beard.

'Take me to Mama,' I begged, as I ran out of the doorway and down the flight of concrete steps. At the last step, someone caught me by the belt of my coat.

'We can't take you yet, not yet, Caithleen,' Mr Gentleman said, and I thought that they were all very cruel, and I couldn't understand why.

'Why? Why? I want to go to her,' I said, trying to escape from his grip. I had so much strength that I could have run the whole five-mile journey to Tintrim.

'For God's sake, tell the girl,' Hickey said.

'Shut up, Hickey,' Mr Brennan shouted, and moved me over to the edge of the kerb where there were several motor-cars. There were people gathering round the motorcars and everyone was talking and mumbling in the dark. Martha helped me into the back of their car, and just before she slammed the door I heard two voices in the Street talking, and one voice said, 'He left five children.'

'Who left five children?' I said to Martha, clutching her by the wrists. I sobbed and said her name and begged her to tell me.

'Tom O'Brien, Caithleen. He's drowned. In his boat, and, and ...' She would rather be struck dumb than tell me, but I knew it by her face.

'And Mama?' I asked. She nodded her poor head and put her arms round me. Mr Brennan got into the front seat just then and started the car.

'She knows,' Martha said to him, between her sobs, but after that I heard nothing, because you hear nothing, nor no one, when your whole body cries and cries for the thing it has lost. Lost. Lost. And yet I could not believe that my mother was gone; and still I knew it was true because I had a feeling of doom and every bit of me was frozen stiff.

'Are we going to Mama?' I said.

'In a while Caithleen; we have to get something first,' they told me as they helped me out of the car and led me into the Greyhound Hotel. Mrs O'Shea kissed me and put me sitting in one of the big leather armchairs that sloped backwards. The room was full of people. Hickey came over and sat on the arm of my chair. He sat on a white linen antimacassar, but no one cared.

'She's not dead,' I said to him, pleading, beseeching.

'They're missing since five o'clock. They left Tuohey's

shop at a quarter to five. Poor Tom O'Brien had two bags of groceries,' Hickey said. Once Hickey said it, it was true. Slowly my knees began to sink from me and everything inside of me was gone. Mr Brennan gave me brandy from a spoon, and then he made me swallow two white pills with a cup of tea.

'She doesn't believe it,' I heard one of the Connor girls say, and then Baba came in and ran over to kiss me.

'I'm sorry about the bloody aul song,' she said.

'Bring the child home,' Jack Holland said, and when I heard him I jumped off the chair, and shouted that I wanted to go to my mother. Mrs O'Shea blessed herself and someone put me sitting down again.

'Caithleen, we're waiting to get news from the barracks,' Mr Gentleman said. He was the only one that could keep me calm.

'I never want to go home again. Never,' I said to him.

'You won't go home, Caithleen,' he said and for a second it seemed that he was going to say, 'Come home to us,' but he didn't. He went over to where Martha was standing beside the sideboard and spoke to her, Then they beckoned to Mr Brennan and he crossed the room to them.

'Where is *he*, Hickey? I don't want to see him.' I was referring to my father.

'You won't see him. He's in hospital in Galway. Passed out when they told him. He was singing in a pub in Portumna when a guard came in to tell him.'

'I'm never going home,' I said to Hickey. His eyes were popping out of his head. He wasn't used to whiskey. Someone had put a tumbler of it in his hand. Everyone was drinking to try and get over the shock. Even Jack Holland took a glass of port wine. The room was thick with cigarette smoke, and

I wanted to go out of it, to go out and find Mama, even to go out and find her dead body. It was all too unreal in there and my head was swimming. The ashtrays were overflowing and the room was hot and smoky. Mr Brennan came over to talk to me. He was crying behind his thick lenses. He said my mother was a lady, a true lady; and that everyone loved her.

'Bring me to her,' I asked. I was no longer wild. My strength had been drained from me.

'We're waiting, Caithleen. We're waiting for news from the barracks. I'll go up there now and see if anything's happened. They're searching the river.' He put out his hands, humbly, in a gesture that seemed to say, 'There's nothing any of us can do now.'

'You're staying with us,' he said, as he lifted wild pieces of hair out of my eyes and smoothed them back gently.

'Thank you,' I said, and he went off to the barracks which was hundred yards up the road. Mr Gentleman went with him.

'That bloody boat was rotten. I always said it,' Hickey said, getting angry with the whole world for not having listened to him.

'Can you come outside, Caithleen? It's confidential,' Jack Holland said as he leaned over the back of my chair. I got up, slowly; and though I cannot remember it, I must have walked across the room to the white door. Most of the paint had been scraped off it. He held it while I went out to the hall. He led me into the back of the hall, where a candle guttered in a saucer. His face was only a shadow. He whispered:

'So help me God, I couldn't do it.'

'Do what, Jack?' I asked. I didn't care. I thought I might

get sick or suffocate. The pills and the brandy were gone to my head.

'Give her the money. Jesus, my hands are tied. The old woman owns everything.' The old woman was his mother. She sat on a rocking-chair beside the fire and Jack had to feed her bread and milk because her hands were crippled with rheumatism.

'God, I'd have done anything for your mama; you know that,' and I said that I did.

Upstairs in a bedroom two greyhounds moaned. It was the moan of death. Suddenly I knew that I had to accept the fact that my mother was dead. And I cried as I have never cried at any other time in my life. Jack cried with me and wiped his nose on the sleeve of his coat.

Then the hall door was pushed in, and Mr Brennan came in.

'No news, Caithleen, no news, love. Come on home to bed,' he said, and he called Martha and Baba out of the room.

'We'll try later,' he said to Mr Gentleman. It was a clear, starry night as we walked across the road to the car. We were home in a few minutes and Mr Brennan made me drink hot whiskey and gave me a yellow capsule. Martha helped me take off my clothes, and when I knelt down to say one prayer, I said, 'Oh God, please bring Mama back to life.' I said it many times but I knew that it was hopeless.

I slept with Baba in one of her nightdresses. Her bed was softer than the one at home. When I turned on my left side she turned too. She put her arm round my stomach and held my hand.

'You're my best friend,' she said in the darkness. And then after a minute she whispered, 'Are you asleep?'

'No.'

'Are you afraid?'

'Afraid of what?'

'That she'll appear,' and when she said it I started to shiver. What is it about death that we cannot bear to have someone who is dead come back to us? I wanted Mama more than anything in the world and yet if the door had opened and she had entered I would have screamed for Martha and Mr Brennan. We heard a noise downstairs, a thud, and we both hid completely under the covers and she said it was death knocks. 'Get Declan,' I said, under the sheet and the blankets.

'No, you go over for him.' But neither of us dared to open the door and go out on the landing. My mother's ghost was waiting for us at the top of the stairs, in a white nightdress.

The pillowslip under me and the white counterpane were wet when I wakened up. Molly wakened me with a cup of tea and toast. She helped me sit up in the bed and fetched my cardigan off the back of a chair. Molly was only two years older than me and yet she fussed over me as if she were my mother.

'Are you sick, love?' she asked. I said that I was hot, and she went off to call Mr Brennan.

'Sir, come here for a second. I want you. I think she has a fever,' and he came and put his hand on my forehead and told Molly to phone the doctor.

They gave me pills all that day and Martha sat in the room and painted her nails and polished them with a little buffer. It was raining, so I couldn't see out the window because it got all fogged up but Martha said it was a terrible day. The phone rang sometime after lunch and Martha kept saying 'Yes, I'll tell her' and 'Too bad' and 'Well, I suppose that's that', and then she came up and told me that they had dragged the great Shannon lake but they hadn't found them; she didn't say that they had given up but I knew they had, and I knew that Mama would never have a grave for me to put flowers on. Somehow she was more dead then than anyone I had ever heard of. I cried again and Martha gave me a sip of wine from her glass and she made me lie back while she read me a story from a magazine. 'Twas a sad story, so I cried worse. It was the last day of childhood.

6

That summer passed quickly. I stayed in Baba's house and went over home in the day-time to get the dinner and wash up. Some days I made the beds. Hickey moved upstairs since Mama's death (we always referred to it as death, not drowning), and the rooms were very untidy. They were sad too with the smell of dust and old socks and a staleness that comes from never opening the windows.

They were over in the fields most days, cutting the corn and binding it into stooks, and I used to go over with bottles of tea at four o'clock. My father ate very little that summer and every time he drank tea he swallowed two aspirins with it. He was quiet and his eyelids were red and swollen. When they came in Hickey milked the cows and my father drank more tea, took off his shoes in the kitchen, and went off to bed. I think he must have cried in bed, because it was too bright to sleep, and anyhow Hickey made a lot of noise downstairs banging milk-cans about and no one could sleep through it.

One day I was upstairs clearing out Mama's drawers and putting her good clothes in a box to send to her sister, when he came upstairs. I hadn't spoken to him very much since he came home from the hospital. I preferred not to.

'There's a little matter you ought to know,' he said. He

had just come in from the village and he was loosening the knot of his tie. I thought for one awful minute that he was drunk, because he looked so dishevelled.

'The place has to go,' he said flatly.

'Go where?' I asked.

He shoved his hat back on his head and began to scratch his forehead. He hesitated. 'There was a bit of debt and with one thing and another it got bigger. I hadn't such luck with the horses. Oh well, we didn't make ends meet.'

'And who's buying it?' I remembered Jack Holland's warning to me about our place being endangered.

'What?' my father asked. He heard me quite well but this was a trick of his when he didn't want to answer. He was narrowing his eyes now, giving that shrewd look to make it seem that he was an astute man. I asked again. I wasn't afraid of him when he was sober.

'The bank practically owns it,' he said at last.

'And who'll run it?' I couldn't believe that someone else other than Hickey would plough and milk and clip the hedge in the summer evenings.

'Jack Holland will probably buy it.'

'Jack Holland!' I was appalled. The rogue. He would get it cheaply. All his palaver about kings and queens and his promising me a new fountain-pencil before I went away to the convent. And to think that he got seven Masses said for Mama. He sent money to a special Order of Priests in Dublin for a bouquet of Masses.

'Where will you go?' I asked. I was thinking of the awful luck if he followed me to the town where the convent was.

'Well, I'm all right. I have a little bit of land for myself and I'll be able to live in the gate-lodge.' The way he spoke anyone would think he had done a smart bit of manipulation

in securing the old, disused gate-lodge behind the rhododendron bushes. It was damp and the front door and two
small windows were choked with briars.

'And Hickey?'

'He'll have to go, I'm afraid. There's no more work for
him.' It was impossible. Hickey had been with us twenty
years, he was there before I was born. He was too fat to go
anywhere else and I told my father this. But he shook his
head. He didn't like Hickey and he was ashamed of all that
had happened.

'What are you doing?' he asked, looking down at the little
neat piles of clothes that were spread around the floor.

'Poor Mama, the poor aul creature,' he said and he went
over to the window and cried.

I didn't want a scene, so I said as if he weren't crying, 'I'll
have to get a uniform before going away and shoes and six
pairs of black stockings.'

'And how much will that be?' he asked, turning round.
There were tears on his cheeks and he snuffled a bit.

'I don't know. Ten or fifteen pounds.' He took out notes
from his pocket and gave me three flyers. The bank must
have given him some money.

'I never deprived you of anything, nor your mother either.
Now did I?'

'No.'

'Ye had only to mention a thing and ye got it.' I said
that was true and went downstairs immediately to fry him
a rasher and make a cup of tea. I called him when it was
ready and he came down in his old clothes. He wasn't
going out any more, the temptation to drink was over for
this time.

'Will you write to me, when you go away?' he asked,

dipping a biscuit into the hot tea. He had taken his teeth out and could only eat a softened biscuit.

'I will.' I was standing with my back to the range.

'Don't forget your poor father,' he said. He put out his arm and tried to draw me over on to his knee, but I pretended not to know what he was doing and ran off to the yard to call Hickey for his tea. He was gone upstairs to bed when I came back and Hickey and I fried some cold cabbage with the rashers and it was delicious. We ate it with mustard. Hickey was a great one for making mustard. Five of the six egg-cups had hardened mustard in them. He blended a fresh lot each day in a clean egg-cup.

Baba was having a birthday party that night, so I asked Hickcy for a bottle of cream so that she would have it with the jelly we had made. He skimmed the two buckets of milk and with his fingers tipped the cream into a can. He wasn't supposed to. Our milk at the creamery next day would have a very low fat content.

'Good-bye, Hickey.'

'Good-bye, sweetheart.' Bull's-Eye came with me over across the fields. It was a short cut to Baba's house. Passing the lower cornfield I stood for a minute to admire it. It was high and ripe and golden, and here and there where it had lodged the jackdaws were feeding. It had a sunlight of its own. The sun was shining from it and the ears stirred in the light sun-gold wind. I sat down on the ditch for a minute. I remembered the day Hickey ploughed that field, we went over with tea and several thick hunks of buttered bread. And later the little green threads came shooting through the red-brown earth and the jackdaws came. Mama loaned one of her beaded hats to put on the scarecrow. I could see her walking over the field with the hat self-consciously laid on her head. Sometimes a sharp and sudden memory of her came to me, and to ease the pain I cried. Bull's-Eye sat on his tail and looked at me while I cried. Then, when I stood up, he came another few yards with me and stopped. He was loyal to Dada, he went back home.

There were five bicycles inside the gate of Baba's house, and the curtains in the front room were drawn. The radiogram was playing – '... where women are women, and French perfume that rocks the room' – and there was a lot of laughing and talking besides. I knew she wouldn't hear me if I knocked, so I went round and tapped at the side window. It was a French window that opened out on to the path. Baba opened it. She was smoking madly, and was dressed in a new blue dress with gorgeous puff sleeves.

'Jesus, I thought you were some yahoo coming for my aul fella,' she said suddenly. She had been nice to me for several weeks since Mama died but when there were other girls around she always made little of me. Declan danced past the window with Gertie Tuohey in his arms. Her black ringlets, like fat sausages, fell down on to her shoulders. Declan had a paper hat on the side of his head and he winked at me.

'Jesus, we're having a whale of a time. I'm delighted you're not here. Go home to hell and make stirabout,' Baba said.

I thought for a minute that she was joking, so I said, very gently, 'I brought the cream.'

'Gimme,' she said, stretching her arm for it. She was wearing a silver bracelet of Martha's. Her arm was grownup and had a bloom of little golden hairs on it.

'Be off, trash,' she said and she shut the window and drew the white bawneen curtain across. Inside I could hear her splitting with laughter.

I didn't go round and let myself in the back door because

I knew that Martha was gone with her husband to see *For Whom the Bell Tolls* in Limerick, and that Baba would have me helping Molly cut sandwiches and make tea all night; so I came back home for an hour.

Hickey was carving his name with a nail on the chicken-house. Dada had told him, so he was leaving traces of himself behind to be remembered by.

'Where will you go, Hickey?'

'I'll go to England. I was going anyhow soon as you went.' Even though he sounded cheerful he looked sad.

'Are you lonesome?'

'Lonesome for what? Not at all. I'll have twenty quid a week and a mott in Birmingham' – but he was lonesome all right.

'What brought you back?' he asked. I told him.

'She's a ringing divil, that one,' he said and I was delighted.

He said that he would clip the hedge, and he thanked God that it would be his last time. He made quick snips with the shears and I collected the pieces and put them into a wheelbarrow. He clipped it right down to the brown twigs and it looked very bare and cold. The wind would come through it now. Where it was very thick in one corner he made a figure of an armchair and I sat in it to see if I would fall through it. I didn't. Then we emptied the wheelbarrow up in the old cellar, and we shut the hens in. Bull's-Eye was already gone to bed in the turf-house. It was unnatural to see Bull's-Eye and Dada going to bed on these lovely still golden evenings. Dada's blind was drawn so I didn't go up to see him, though I knew he would have liked a cup of tea. I hated going into his room when he was in bed. I could see Mama on the pillow beside him. Reluctant and frightened as if something terrible were being done to her. She used to sleep with me as often as she could and only went across to his room when he made her. He wore no pyjamas in bed, and I was ashamed even to think of it.

The old white beehive was still there, in the corner of the kitchen garden. Two of the legs had come off so that it sagged a little to one side.

'What'll you do with the beehive?' I asked Hickey. A few years before that he had decided to keep bees. He thought he would get very rich by selling the honey to all the local people; and he made the hive himself in the evenings, after work. Then he got a swarm of heather-honey bees out in the mountain, and he was very excited about all the money he was going to make. But like everything else it failed. The bees stung him and he roared and yelled in the kitchen garden and made Mama get him a hot poultice. For some reason or another he never got any honey and he got rid of the bees by smothering them.

'What'll you do with it?' I asked again.

'Let it rot,' he said. His voice was somewhat weary, and I think he sighed, because he knew what failures we all were. The place was gone, Mama was gone: the flag was white with hen-dirt and there were thistles and ragwort covering every inch of the front lawn.

'I'll convey you,' said Hickey and he linked me as we walked down the field in the dusk. It was chilly and the cows were lying under the trees with their eyes wide open, staring at us. Dogs barked in the distance. The grass was quiet and two bats flew in front of us.

'Don't grow up to be a snotty-nose now, when you go to that convent,' he said.

'I'm afraid of Baba; she makes so little of me, Hickey.'

"'Tis a kick in the backside she wants, the little upstart. I'd give her something to make her afraid.' But he didn't say what.

'I'll send you an odd bob from England,' he said, to cheer me up. He left me at Baba's gate and went down to the Greyhound Hotel to have a few drinks. It was after hours but he preferred drinking then.

Upstairs in Baba's room I took out the three five-pound notes that I had hidden inside my vest since earlier in the evening. They were warm and I hid them under the pillow. I decided to go to Limerick next day to buy my school uniform. When Baba came up she tried to waken me. She plucked at my eyelashes, and tickled my face with the wet stem of a snapdragon. I had brought over a bunch from home and put them in a vase beside the bed.

If I wakened she might find out that I was going to Limerick and she would come with me and spoil my day.

'Declan,' she called her brother from the bathroom.

'Isn't she like a pig asleep?' she said, and drew back the covers so that he could see the full length of my body. I felt chilly when she did that and drew my feet up under my nightdress.

'She snores like a bloody sow,' she said, and I almost sat up and called her a liar. Next thing, the two of them were boxing and Declan knocked her on to the floor while she yelled for Molly.

'Say that again. Say that again,' he said, holding one of my shoes over her. I could see them by peering through my eye-lashes. Declan was my friend that night.

After she got into bed, Baba kept saying: 'She's coming. She's appearing. She's coming back to tell you to give me all her jewellery.' But no matter what she said I stayed perfectly still and kept my eyes closed.

The moon shone in on us and there was a streak of silver light across the carpeted floor. I slept badly and when the grandfather clock struck seven I got out of bed and carried my clothes off to the bathroom. I forgot my money and I had to go back for it. Her black hair was spread out on the pillow and she stirred a little when I was coming away. 'Cait, Cait,' she called me, but I didn't answer her. She must have gone to sleep, because I came down to the kitchen and dressed there in front of the Aga cooker. I was delighted to be going off for the whole day, away from everybody.

7

I was standing outside the gate waiting for the bus when
Mr Gentleman's car passed by and went up the street. It
stopped outside the garage on the hill for petrol, then he
turned round and came back.

'Are you going somewhere, Caithleen?' he asked, winding down the window. I said that I was going to Limerick
and he said to sit in, So I sat on the black leather seat
beside him and my heart fluttered. The moment I heard
him speak and the moment I looked at his eyes my heart
always fluttered. His eyes were tired or sad or something.
He smoked little cigars and threw the butts out the
window.

'Are they horrible?' I asked. I had to say something.

'Here, try one,' he said, and he took the cigar out of his
mouth and handed it to me. I was thinking of his mouth, of
the shape of it, and the taste of his tongue, while I had one
short, self-conscious puff. I began to cough at once. I said it
was worse than horrible, and he laughed. He drove very
fast.

We parked the car down a side street and I thanked him
and went off. He was locking the door. I hated leaving him.
There was something about him that made me want to be
with him. He called me back. 'What about lunch, Caithleen?'

I intended having tea and cream-buns but I didn't tell him that.

'Would you like to meet me?'

I said that I would. His eyes were still sad but I was singing as I came away.

'You won't forget, will you?'

'No, Mr Gentleman, I won't forget.' I hurried off to the shops.

I went into the biggest shop on the main street. Mama always shopped there. I asked a woman who was down on her knees scrubbing the floor where I'd go for a gym frock.

'Fourth floor, love. Take the lift.' She had no teeth when she smiled. I gave her a shilling. I had saved three shillings on my bus fare. I could afford to be extravagant.

I got into the lift. A small boy with a buttoned tunic operated it.

'I want a gym frock,' I said. He ignored me.

I sat on a stool in the corner, because it was my first time in a lift and I felt dizzy. We passed three floors with a click at each floor; then it clicked, stopped, and he let me out. The gym-frock counter was directly opposite and I went across.

Afterwards I weighed myself in the cloakroom and learnt that I was seven pounds too light. There was a chart printed on the side of the scales that gave the correct weight for each person's height.

I went down the stairs. The carpet was worn but it was soft under the feet. In the basement I bought presents for everybody. A scarf for Dada, a penknife for Hickey, a boat-shaped bottle of perfume for Baba, and pink hand-jelly for Martha. Then I came out on to the street and looked in a jewellery window. I saw a lot of watches that I liked. I went into a big church at the corner, to have three wishes. We were told that we had three wishes whenever we went into a new church. The holy water wasn't in a font like at home, but there was a drop at the end of a narrow tap, and I put my finger under it and blessed myself. I wished that Mama was in Heaven, that my father would never drink again, and that Mr Gentleman would not forget to come at one o'clock.

I came to the hotel a half an hour before the time so that I wouldn't miss him, and I was afraid to go inside to the hall in case a porter should tell me that I had no right to be there.

He had had a haircut, and as he came up the steps his face looked sharp and I could see the tops of his ears. Before that they were hidden under a soft fall of fine grey hair. He smiled at me. My heart fluttered once again and I found it hard to speak.

'Men prefer to kiss young girls without lipstick, you know,' he said. He was referring to the two thin lines of pink lipstick that I had put on. I bought a tube in Woolworth's and went round to the mirror counter and applied it in front of a mirror that showed up all the pores on my face.

'I wasn't thinking of kissing. I never kiss anyone,' I said.

'Never?' He was teasing me. I knew by the way he smiled.

'No. Nobody. Only Hickey.'

'Nobody else?' I shook my head and he caught my elbow as we went into the dining-room. My arms were thin and white and I was ashamed of them.

It was my first time in a city hotel. I decided to have the cheapest thing on the menu.

'I'll have Irish stew,' I said.

'No, you will not,' he replied. He was cross but it wasn't real crossness, only pretending. He ordered little chickens for both of us. Another waiter brought a tall, slender, dark-green bottle of wine. There was a bowl of mixed flowers on the table between us, but they had no smell.

He poured some wine into his own glass, sipped it, and smiled. Then he poured some into mine. I had my Confirmation pledge, but I was ashamed to tell him. He was smiling at me all the time. It was a sad smile and I liked it.

'Tell me about your day.'

'I bought my school uniform and I walked around. That's all.'

The wine was bitter. I would have rather'd lemonade. I had ice-cream afterwards, and Mr Gentleman had a white cheese with green threads of mould in it. It smelt like Hickey's socks, not the new socks I bought him but the old ones under his mattress.

'That was lovely,' I said, pushing my plate over to the edge of the table where it would be handy for the waiter to get it.

'It was,' he agreed. I didn't know whether Mr Gentleman was shy, or whether it was that he was just too lazy to talk. Or bored, He was no good for small talk.

'We must have another lunch some day,' he said.

'I'm going away next week,' I replied.

'Going away to America? Too bad we'll never meet one another again.' I think he thought he was being very funny. He drank some more wine and his eyes got very large and very, very wistful. They met mine for as long as I wanted.

'So you tell me that you have never kissed anyone?' he said. He had a way of looking at me that made me feel innocent. He was staring now. Sometimes directly into my pupils, other times his eyes would roam all over my face and settled for a minute on my neck. My neck. My neck was snow-white and I was wearing a silk dress with a curved neckline. It was an ice-blue dress with blossoms on it. Sometimes I thought they were tiny apple blossoms and then again I thought the pattern was one of snow falling; but either way it was a nice dress and the skirt was composed of millions of little pieces that flowed when I walked.

'The next time we have lunch, don't wear lipstick,' he said. 'I prefer you without it.'

The coffee was bitter. I used four lumps of sugar. We came out and went to the pictures. He bought me a box of chocolates with a ribbon on it.

I cried halfway through the picture because there was a sad bit about a boy having to leave a girl in order to go off to war. He laughed when he saw me crying and whispered that we should go out. He took my hand as we went up the dark passage, and out in the vestibule he wiped my eyes and told me to smile.

We drove home while it was still bright. The hills in the distance were blue and the trees in the folds of the hills were a dusty lilac. Farmers were saving hay in fields along the roadside and children were sitting on haycocks eating apples and throwing butts over the ditch. The smell of hay came through the window, half spice, half perfume.

A woman wearing wellingtons was driving cows home to be milked. We had to slow down to let them in a side gate and I caught him looking at me. We smiled at each other and his hand came off the steering-wheel and rested on the lap of my ice-blue dress. My hand was waiting for it. We locked our fingers and for the rest of the journey we drove like that, except going round sharp bends. His hand was small and white and very smooth. There were no hairs on it.

'You're the sweetest thing that ever happened to me,' he

73

said. It was all he said and it was only a whisper. Afterwards, lying in bed in the convent, I used to wonder whether he said it or whether I had imagined it.

He squeezed my hand before I got out of the car. I thanked him and reached into the back seat for my packages. He sighed, as if he were going to say something; but Baba ran out to the car and he slipped away from me.

My soul was alive; enchantment; something I had never known before. It was the happiest day of my whole life.

'Good-bye, Mr Gentleman,' I said through the window. There was an odd expression in his smile which seemed to be saying, 'Don't go.' But he did go, my new god, with a face carved out of pale marble and eyes that made me sad for every woman who hadn't known him.

'What'n the hell are you mooning about?' Baba asked, and I went into the house laughing.

'I bought you a present,' I said, and in my mind I kept singing it, 'You're the sweetest thing that ever happened to me.' It was like having a precious stone in my pocket and I had only to say the words in order to feel it, blue, precious, enchanting ... my deathless, deathless song.

8

The last view I had of home was in the rain. We drove past the gate in Mr Brennan's car, and there was a white horse galloping over the front field.

'Good-bye, Home,' I said, wiping the steam from the inside of the window so that I could wave and have a last look at the rusty iron gate and the avenue of dripping trees.

My handkerchief was wet from crying. I cried all morning. I cried saying good-bye to Hickey and Molly and Maisie at the hotel; and Baba cried too. Baba and I weren't speaking.

Martha sat between us and we each looked out the window at our own side; but there wasn't much more to see – the wind-bent hedges, the melancholy mountains, and wet hens huddled in farmyards.

My father sat in front talking to Mr Brennan.

'This is a good car now. How many miles do you get to the gallon?' my father asked. He called Mr Brennan 'Doc' and lit two cigarettes at a time. He gave one to Mr Brennan. 'Here, Doc.' Mr Brennan mumbled his thanks. He never addressed my father by name.

Martha lit one of her own, out of spite. My father neglected her. He had no interest in women.

I began to worry if I had forgotten anything, and went over the contents of my case. I wondered had I put in the small things, and if there were name-tapes on all my underwear. Baba had printed name-tapes from Dublin, but I wrote my name with marking-ink on strips of white tape, and stitched the tape on to my clothes. I hate stitching, so Molly did most of it for me and I gave her two of Mama's dresses in return. The cake and the two jars of honey Mrs Tuohey gave me were in a travel-bag, and I had Jack Holland's fountain-pencil clipped to the front of my gym frock. I had the doll's tea-set in the travel-bag too. All the little cups and saucers wrapped in separate pieces of tissue paper; and the tea-pot and sugar-bowl were in a nest of chaff. I took the chaff out of the bottom row of Mr Gentleman's box of chocolates. There were only a few sweets in the bottom row, all the rest was chaff. I thought of writing to the makers to complain, because there was a slip of paper which said that people should write in, if they weren't satisfied; but in the end I didn't bother.

The doll's tea-service was the only thing I brought from home. I always liked it. I used to sit and look at it in the china cabinet, just sit there admiring it in the sunlight. It was pale-blue china and it looked very tender and breakable. I mean, even more breakable than ordinary china. Mama gave it to me the Christmas I discovered there was no Santa Claus. At least, the Christmas Baba told me that I was a bloody fool to believe in Santa Claus, when every halfwit knew that it was your damn' mother or father dressed up. When my mother gave me the tea-set I asked if I might put it in the china cabinet. I was very grown-up that way; I never played with toys, nor broke them, nor dismantled them, like other children. I had five dolls, each without a scratch. Mama often put a lump of sugar into one of the little cups as a surprise for me; and every time I lost a tooth I put it in one of these cups at night, and in the morning the tooth was gone and there was a sixpence in its place. Mama said that the fairies left the money when they were dancing down in the room at night.

Remembering these little things made me cry, and my father looked back and said: 'You'd think you were going to America. Sure we'll visit you every few Sundays, won't we, Doc?' I could hardly tell him that I wasn't crying for him. I could hardly say, 'I don't care if you never visit me,' or 'I'll be happier in the convent than at home in the gatelodge, coaxing a fire with damp sticks, and worrying about the whiff of whiskey off your breath.' But I said nothing. I was trying to control my tears and I prayed that I would last the journey without having to root in the case for a clean handkerchief. The case was under Martha's feet.

'Now you two *must* make it up,' Martha said. We looked at one another, and Baba drooped her eyelids until the lashes were fluttering on her cheeks. They were long lashes, like daisy petals dyed coal black. 'Be off, trash,' she said, between her teeth, and she turned away again.

I felt like a crow in my navy serge gym frock and my navy knitted jumper. A woman in the village who owned a knitting machine made it for me as a present. I got a lot of presents after Mama's death. People pitying me, I suppose. My legs were thin and sad in the black cotton stockings, and they were itchy too, because I had been used to wearing no stockings all the summer. I was thin and much too tall for my fourteen years.

'Jesus, they'll say you have worms,' Baba said, the night I

fitted on my uniform. She looked pretty in hers, plump and round. Her curly hair was cut short, her face brown from the sun, and she looked like an autumn nut, brown and smooth.

'What is it, anyhow, between you two?' Martha asked. Neither of us spoke.

'You'll just have to talk when you get there. There won't be anyone else to talk to,' she said. She was right. In the convent we would only have each other.

'We will never speak again, never,' I kept repeating under my breath. Baba had broken my heart, destroyed my life. This was how she had done it.

The night I came home from Limerick, I was gay and happy thinking of my day with Mr Gentleman, smiling to myself as I sat on the bed with my feet curled in under the red satin eiderdown.

'You're very happy in yourself,' Baba said, as she undressed and laid her clothes on the back of the wicker chair. 'Hurry up and get in to bed, this candle is nearly burnt out.'

She was jealous of my happiness.

'I want to sit here all night and dream.' I spoke slowly and, I thought, dramatically.

'Jesus, you're nuts. What's happened to you anyhow?'

'Love,' I said, throwing out my arms in a hopeless, lost gesture.

'Who's the fool?'

'You wouldn't know.'

'Declan?'

'Nonsense,' I replied as if Declan were some little nonentity whom I couldn't even tolerate.

'Hickey?'

'No,' I said. I was enjoying myself.

'Tell me.'

'I can't.'

'Tell me,' she said, tucking the top of her pyjamas into the trousers. 'Tell me, or I'll tickle it out of you,' and she began to tickle me under the arms.

'I will. I will. I will.' I'd do anything not to be tickled. So when I got back my breath I told her.

'No sir, not on your bloody life. It's a lie.'

'It's not a lie. He gave me chocolates, and took me to the pictures. He told me that I was the sweetest thing that ever happened to him. He said the colour of my hair was wonderful, and my eyes were like real pearls and my skin like a peach in the sunlight.' He said none of these things of course, but once 1 started telling lies I couldn't stop.

'Go on, tell me more,' she said. Her mouth was half open with wonder and astonishment and envy.

'You won't tell anyone,' I said, because I was going to tell her the bit about holding my hand. And then all of a sudden I could see that look coming into her eyes. It was a green look, the eyes narrowed like a cat's. I've seen it since a thousand times, in trains, in wedding photographs, and I always say to myself, 'Some poor fool is going to be put through it,' so once again I said, 'You won't tell anyone, Baba?'

'No' – pause – 'only – *Mrs* Gentleman.'

'Don't tell a single solitary person,' I pleaded.

'No – only Mrs Gentleman and Mammy and Daddy and your aul fella.'

'I was only joking,' I lied. 'I never met him. I was only pulling your leg. He just gave me a seat from Limerick. That's all.'

'Really!' she said, trying to raise one eyebrow. 'Well,' she added, blowing out the candle, 'Mammy, Daddy, and I are having dinner with the Gentlemans tomorrow night and I'll mention it to him.'

I undressed in the dark and when I got into bed she had all the blankets pulled over to her side.

'No, don't, don't tell,' I begged, but she was asleep while I was still pleading with her.

Next evening they did have dinner with the Gentlemans, and drove home just before midnight. I was behind the hall door, waiting.

'Not in bed yet, Caithleen?' Mr Brennan said to me as he looked in the address book beside the telephone, to see if there were any night calls. Martha came in with a big bunch of gladioli in her arms, and her eyes were large and smiling.

'No, Mr Brennan,' I said. I curled my finger and beckoned Baba to follow me into the study.

'Baba, I have a present for you, one of Mama's rings the one you like best. The black one.' I gave it to her and she put it on in the dark. There was a diamond in the centre of it, and you could see it sparkle in the faint light that wandered in from the hall lamp.

'You didn't tell,' I said.

'Oh, tell? Oh no, I didn't tell. Old Mrs Gentleman would be over here with a hatchet if I told. But J.W.' (that was Mr Gentleman, she meant) 'and I were having a stroll in the garden and I mentioned you and he said, "Oh that little one, she suffers greatly from her imagination."'

'Impossible,' I said aloud.

'Oh yes. He was linking me around, showing me the various flowers, offering me a bunch of grapes, asking me what I thought of this and that, imploring me to play chess with him, and I mentioned your name and he said, "Oh let's not discuss her," so I dropped the subject. We were out there a hell of a long time, old Ma Gentleman stuck her head out the window finally and said "You two," so we had to come in.'

That finished it. I would never be able to look him in the face again. And to think that I had given her Mama's best ring.

Next morning Baba went to Confession, and at eleven o'clock the phone rang.

Molly came upstairs for me. I was filling in my diary, doleful pieces about Mr Gentleman.

'Mr Gentleman wants you on the phone,' she said, and my heart started to race.

To go down and talk to him was all I desired. But now he was ringing to tell me how vulgar and disgusting I had been, how falsely I had re-described our day together, and I could not endure it.

'Tell him I'm out and that I'll ring him,' I said to Molly. I had some idea that I would write him a beautiful letter, a magnificent letter, most of which I'd copy out of *Wuthering Heights*. I'd wait around, and dart out from behind a tree to hand it to him as he got out to open the gate.

Molly went down and said I was gone to Confession and that she'd tell me soon as I got in. They talked for another minute. I was demented wondering what he'd have to say to Molly, and then she put down the phone.

'Well?' I was hanging over the banister, deathly white, with ink shadows under my eyes. I hadn't slept for two nights.

'He's terrible sorry but he's gone to Paris on a trip,' she said, rolling up her sleeves and showing her fat, pink strong arms to the daylight.

'To Paris?' I thought of girls and sin at once. How dare he?

'Yeh, he had to go sudden, some relative of his is dying,' she said, and she began to attack the hall floor with a scrubbing-brush.

I saw no more of Mr Gentleman, because we left for the convent three days later.

It took me only a second to recall all of this in the motor-car, and then I returned to my wet handkerchief and to Baba offering me a conversation lozenge. It had *Let us be Friends* written on it but I was too bitter to smile.

We got into the convent town at dusk; just outside it there was a lake, a dark sheet of water, and when we drove past it, a bleak wind blew in through the half-open window. Then we drove through a narrow street that had electric lights every fifty yards or so along the pavement and there were poplar trees in between the green metal lamp-posts. The dark sheet of water and the sad poplar trees and the strange dogs outside the strange shops made me indescribably sad.

'Nice place,' my father said, and snuffled. Nice place! A lot he knew about it. How could he think it was a nice place by just looking out the window?

'What about a drink, Bob?' he asked; and Martha, who had been dozing in the back seat, brightened up and said, 'Yes, let's give the children some lemonade.'

We stopped on the main street and went into a hotel. My knees were stiff. There was faded red Turkey carpet on the front hall and on the stairs that rose out of the hall. To the right was a dining-room with lots of little tables laid with white cloths. There were two bottles of ketchup on each table. A red bottle and a brown bottle. We went into a room marked 'Lounge'.

'Well, Bob, what will it be?' my father asked. I was trembling in case he should take anything strong himself.

'Whiskey,' said Mr Brennan, taking off his glasses. They were mizzled with rain and he wiped them with a clean white handkerchief.

'And you, Mam?' my father asked Martha. She hated being called 'Mam'. It was ageing.

'Gin,' she said in an ungracious whisper. She hoped her husband was not listening; but I saw him grind his teeth as he went over to look at a faded hunting picture on the wall.

'I'll have a lemonade, I suppose,' my father said, sighing. He was looking at me. He wanted me to acknowledge him, to give him a glance that told him he was brave and strong and good. But I looked the other way, preoccupied with my own miseries. In my mind I could see Mr Gentleman's hand on the steering-wheel, and his gaze as he turned from the windscreen to look at me when the car slowed down to the cows in the gateway.

Baba had grapefruit. To be different, I thought resentfully. We didn't sit down because we were in a hurry. We had to report at the convent before seven. There was a nice turf fire in the big red-brick fireplace and I hated leaving the hotel. My father paid for the drinks and we left.

The convent was a grey stone building with hundreds of small square curtainless windows like so many eyes spying out on the wet sinful town. There were green railings round it and high green gates that led to a dark cypress avenue. My father got out of the car to open the gates, and gave the door a god-awful bang. Mr Brennan winced and I was ashamed that my father didn't know better.

We parked the car under a tree and got out. We went down a flight of stone steps and crossed a concrete yard towards an open door. In the hallway a nun came forward to meet us. She wore a black, loose-fitting habit and a black veil over her head. Framing her face, and covering her fore-head, her ears, and her chest was a stiff white thing which they call a gamp. It almost covered her eyebrows but you could just barely see the tips of them. They were black and they met in the middle over the bridge of her red nose. Her face was shiny.

My father took off his hat and told her who we were. Mr Brennan followed in with the cases.

'You're welcome,' she said to Baba and myself. Her hand was cold.

'Well, Baba, try to behave yourself,' Mr Brennan said doubtfully to Baba. Martha kissed me and put two coins into my hand. I said 'Oh no,' but as I was saying it my fingers closed over them gratefully. Reluctantly I kissed my father and I clung for a second to Mr Brennan and tried to thank him but I was too embarrassed.

The nun smiled all through her farewells. She had been watching others since early morning.

'They will settle down,' she said. Her voice was deter-mined though not harsh; but when she said 'They will settle down' she seemed to be saying 'They must settle down.'

Our parents left. I thought of them going off to have tea

84

and mixed grill in the warm hotel and I could taste the hot pepper taste of Yorkshire relish.

'Well now,' said the nun, taking a man's silver watch out of her pocket. 'First your tea. Follow me,' and we followed her down a long hallway. It had red tiles on the floor and there were shiny white tiles half-way up the walls. On each tiled window-ledge there was a castor-oil plant and at the bottom of the hall there was a row of oak presses. It was like a hospital, but it smelt of wax polish instead of an-aesthetics. It was scrupulously and frighteningly clean. Dirt can be consoling and friendly in a strange place, I thought.

We hung our coats in the cloakroom and she helped us find a compartment in the press where our names were already written and where we were to store caps, gloves, shoes, boot polish, prayer-books, and small things like that. The press was like a honeycomb and not all the compart-ments were filled yet.

We followed her across another concrete yard to the refectory. She walked busily and the thick black rosary beads, hanging from her waist, swung outwards as she walked. We went into a big room with a high ceiling and long wooden tables stretching lengthwise. There were benches at either side of the tables.

The big girls, or the 'senior' girls, sat at one table and they were talking furiously. Talking about the holidays and the times they had. I suppose a lot of them were inventing things that never happened, just to make themselves import-ant. Most of them had their hair freshly washed and one or two were very pretty. I picked out the pretty ones at once. At the junior table the new girls were strangers to one another. They looked lost and mopey, and cried quietly to themselves.

We were put sitting opposite one another and Baba smiled across at me, but we still hadn't spoken. A little nun poured us two cups of tea from a big white enamel tea-pot. She was so small I thought she'd drop the teapot. She wore a white muslin apron over her black habit. The apron meant that she was a lay nun. The lay nuns did the cooking and cleaning and scrubbing; and they were lay nuns because they had no money or no education when they entered the convent. The other nuns were called choir nuns. I didn't know that then but one of the senior girls explained it to me. Her name was Cynthia and she taught me a lot of things.

The bread was already buttered and a dopey girl next to me kept passing me a plate of dull grey bread.

'It looks awful,' I said and shook my head. I had cake in my case and knew that I would eat some later on. She passed me the plate twice more and Baba sniggered. After tea we trooped up to the convent chapel to say the rosary aloud.

It was a pretty chapel and there were pale pink roses on the altar. The nuns sang during Benediction. One nun sang like a lark. Her voice was different from all the others, singing 'Mother, Mother, I am Coming', and I cried for my own mother. I thought of the day when we sat in the kitchen and saw the lark take the specks of sheep's wool off the barbed wire and carry it off to build her nest.

'Will you be a nun when you're big?' Mama asked me. She would have liked me to be a nun, it was better than marrying. Anything was, she thought.

That first evening in the chapel was strange and emotional. The incense floated down the nave, followed by the articulate voice of the priest, who knelt before the altar in a gold-crusted cloak.

We knelt in the back of the chapel on wooden benches, and there were wood rails separating us from where the nuns knelt. The nuns were one in front of the other in little oak compartments that were fixed to the walls on either side. They all looked alike from the back except the postulants who wore lace bonnets and whose hair showed through the lace.

We all filed out of the chapel, making as much noise as twenty horses galloping over a stony road. Some girls had studs in their shoes and you could hear the studs scratching the tiled floor of the chapel porch. We went down to the recreation hall where Sister Margaret was sitting on a rostrum, waiting to speak to us. She welcomed the new girls, re-welcomed the old ones, and gave a quick summary of the convent rules:

'Silence in the dormitory, and at breakfast.
Shoes to be taken off before going into the dormitory.
No food to be kept in presses in the dormitory.
To bed within twenty minutes after you go upstairs.'

'Now,' she said, 'will the girls who wish to have milk at night, please put up their hands?' I had a bad chest, so I put up my hand and committed myself to a lukewarm cup of dusty milk every night; and committed my father to a bill for two pounds a year. Scholarships did not cater for bad chests.

We went to bed early.

Our dormitory was on the first floor. There was a lavatory on the landing outside it, and twenty or thirty girls were queueing there, hopping from one foot to another as if they couldn't wait. I took off my shoes and carried them into the dormitory. It was a long room with windows on either side, and a door at the far end. Over the door was a large crucifix, and there were holy pictures along the yellow distempered walls. There were two rows of iron beds down the length of the room. They were covered with white cotton counterpanes and the iron was painted white as well. The beds were numbered and I found mine easily enough. Baba was six beds away from me. At least it was nice to know that she was near, in case we should ever speak. There were three radiators along the wall but they were cold.

I sat down on the chair beside my bed, took off my garters, and peeled my stockings off slowly. The garters were too tight and they had made marks on my legs. I was looking at the red marks, worrying in case I'd have varicose veins before morning; and I didn't know that Sister Margaret was standing right behind me. She wore rubber-soled shoes and she had a way of stealing up on one. I jumped off the chair when she said, 'Now, girls.' I turned round to face her. Her eyes were cross and I could see a small cist on one of her irises. She was that near to me.

'The new girls won't know this, but our convent has always been proud of its modesty. Our girls, above anything else, are good and wholesome and modest. One expression of modesty is the way a girl dresses and undresses. She should do so with decorum and modesty. In an open dormitory like this ...' she paused, because someone had come in the bottom door and had bashed a ewer against the woodwork. Even my ear-lobes were blushing. She went on: 'Upstairs the senior girls have separate cubicles; but, as I say, in an open dormitory like this, girls are requested to dress and undress under the shelter of their dressing-gowns. Girls should face the foot of the bed, doing this, as they might surprise each other if they face the side of the bed.' She coughed and went off twiddling a bunch of keys in the air. She unlocked the oak door at the end of the room and went inside.

The girl allotted to the bed next to mine raised her eyes to heaven. She had squint eyes and I didn't like her. Not because of the squint but because she looked like someone who would have bad taste about everything. She was wearing a pretty, expensive dressing-gown and rich fluffy slippers; but you felt that she bought them to show off, and not because they were pretty. I saw her put two bars of chocolate under her pillow.

Trying to undress under a dressing-gown is a talent you must develop. Mine fell off six or seven times, but finally I managed to keep it on by stooping very low.

I was rooting in my travel-bag when the lights went out. Small figures in nightdresses hurried up the carpeted passage and disappeared into the cold white beds.

I wanted to get the cake that was in the bottom of my bag. The tea-service was on top, so I took it out piece by piece. Baba crept up to the foot of my bed and for the first time we talked, or rather, we whispered.

'Jesus, 'tis hell,' she said. 'I won't stick it for a week.'

'Nor me. Are you hungry?'

'I'd eat a young child,' she said. I was just getting my nail-file out of my toilet-bag, to cut a hunk of cake with, when the key was turned in the door at the end of the room. I covered the cake quickly with a towel and we stood there perfectly still, as Sister Margaret came towards us, holding her flash-lamp.

'What is the meaning of this?' she asked. She knew our names already and addressed us by our full names, not just

Bridget (Baba's real name) and Caithleen; but Bridget Brennan and Caithleen Brady.

'We were lonely, Sister,' I said.

'You are not alone in your loneliness. Loneliness is no excuse for disobedience.' She was speaking in a penetrating whisper. The whole dormitory could hear her.

'Go back to your bed, Bridget Brennan,' she said. Baba tripped off quietly. Sister Margaret shone the flash-lamp to and fro, until the beam caught the little tea-service on the bed.

'What is this?' she asked, picking up one of the cups.

'A tea-service, Sister. I brought it because my mother died.' It was a stupid thing to say and I regretted it at once. I'm always saying stupid things, because I don't think before I say them.

'Sentimental childish conduct,' she said. She lifted the outside layer of her black habit and shaped it into a basket. Then she put the tea-service in there and carried it off.

I got in between the icy sheets and ate a piece of seed cake. The whole dormitory was crying. You could hear the sobbing and choking under the covers. Smothered crying.

The head of my bed backed on to the head of another girl's bed; and in the dark a hand came through the rungs and put a bun on my pillow. It was an iced bun and there was something on top of the icing. Possibly a cherry. I gave her a piece of cake and we shook hands. I wondered what she looked like, as I hadn't noticed her when the lights were on. She was a nice girl whoever she was. The bun was nice too. Two or three beds away I heard some girl munch an apple under the covers. Everyone seemed to be eating and crying for their mothers.

My bed faced a window and I could see a sprinkling of

stars in one small corner of the sky. It was nice to lie there watching the stars, waiting for them to fade or to go out, or to flare up into one brilliant firework. Waiting for something to happen in the deathly, unhappy silence.

9

We were wakened at six next morning. The angelus bell was ringing from the convent tower when Sister Margaret came in chanting the morning offering. She put on the lights and I was up and staggering on my feet before I even knew where I was.

She told us to wash and dress quickly. Mass was in fifteen minutes.

Drawing a comb, limply, through my tangled hair, I saw that Baba was still in bed. Poor Baba, she could never waken in the mornings. I went down and dragged her out. She yawned and rubbed her eyes and asked: 'Where are we and what time is it?' I told her. She said, 'Jesus wept!' It was her new phrase, instead of just plain 'Jesus'. Her face was pale and sad and she couldn't open the knots in her shoe-laces.

We were the last to leave the dormitory. The prefect had put the lights out. It was rather dark and we had to grope to find our way up the passage and down the steep wooden stairs that led to the recreation hall. There were birds singing in the convent trees as we crossed the tarmac drive-way to the chapel. The birds reminded us both of the same thing. Home wasn't such a bad place after all.

Mass had started when we got in, so we knelt on the

kneeler nearest the door, but there was no bench for us to sit on.

'We'll get housemaid's knee from this,' Baba whispered.

'What's that?'

'It's a disease. All nuns have it from kneeling.' A senior girl turned round and gave us an eye that told us to shut up. My mind wandered all through Mass. The dandruff on girls' gym frocks, the sun coming through the stained-glass window; the shadows where nuns knelt. Nuns with heads bowed humbly, nuns kneeling upright, older nuns kneeling slackly, resting a little on their haunches. I wondered if I would ever get to know them from their backs. A nun served Mass too. It was funny to hear her thin voice answering the priest in Latin.

Her name was Sister Mary and the priest's name was Father Thomas. Cynthia told me on the way out.

'You're new. Do you like it?' she asked, as she overtook us going down the steps. She ignored Baba.

'It's awful,' I said.

'You'll get used to it. It's not so bad.'

'I'm lonesome.'

'For whom? Your mammy?'

'No. She's dead.'

'Oh, poor you,' she said, putting her arm round my waist. She promised to take care of me. The big girls always took care of the new ones, and Cynthia was going to take care of me. I liked her. She was a tall girl with yellow hair and small alert brown eyes. She bad a bust too. A thing no other girl in the convent dared have. But Cynthia was different, because she was half Swedish and her mother was a convert.

First we had drill in the open yard that looked out on the street. There were school walls on three sides of it, and there were railings at the fourth side dividing us from the street. Near the railings was an open shed where the day-girls kept their bicycles. The day-girls were those whose parents lived in the town and they came in and out to school every day. Cynthia told me that they were all very obliging. She meant that they would post letters on the sly for me, or bring sweets from the shops.

'Arms forward. Arms to toes. Don't bend knees,' Sister Margaret said. You could hear knees crack and breaths gasping. Seventy bottoms were humped up in the air and I could see the white thighs of girls in front of me. That space where their black stocking tops ended which the legs of their knickers did not cover.

'Jesus, it's worse than the army,' Baba said to me. Her voice came from upside down, because our heads were near the ground.

'Winter and summer,' a girl next to us said.

'Silence, please,' said Sister Margaret. She was standing on her toes, counting ten. And while we waited, a boy with milkcans went by whistling. His whistle was sweeter than the notes of a flute. Sweeter, because he didn't know how happy he had made us. All of us. He reminded us of our lives at borne. We went in to breakfast.

We had tea and buttered bread and there was a spoon of marmalade on each girl's plate. We began to talk furiously.

'Thanks for the cake,' said a girl across the table. She had black hair, a fringe, and pale, freckled skin.

'Oh, it's you?' I said. She was nice. Not pretty or flashy or anything but nice. Sisterly.

'Where are you from?' she asked, and I told her.

'I have a scholarship,' I said. It was better to tell it myself than have Baba tell it.

'God, you must be a genius,' she said, frowning.

'Not at all,' I said. But I liked the praise. It warmed me inside.

'I'm having visitors Sunday week. I'll get more cakes and things,' she said. I was just going to say something very friendly to her, because after all she was next to me in the dormitory, and she was likely to get lots of cakes; but Sister Margaret came in, clapping her hands.

'Silence,' she said. Her words seemed to remain in the room, hanging over our heads. She began to read from her spiritual book. She read a story about Saint Teresa and how Teresa worked in a laundry and let the soap spatters into her eyes as an act of mortification.

'Don't let the soap get in your eyes,' Baba hummed quietly to herself and I was terrified lest she should be heard.

'I'll drink Lysol or any damn' thing to get out of here,' she said to me on the way out. A man, at home, had poisoned himself that way. Sister Margaret walked past us and gave us a bitter and suspicious eye. But she hardly overheard us, or we would have been expelled then.

'I'd rather be a Protestant,' Baba said.

'They have convents too,' I said, sighing.

'Not like this gaol,' she replied. She was almost crying.

We went up to the dormitory and Cynthia was waiting for me on the first landing.

'That's for you,' she said, handing me a holy picture for my prayer-book. She ran off quickly. In purple ink it had written: *To my new lovely friend, from her loving Cynthia.*

'That sort of mush gives me acidosis,' Baba said, sneering. She went in ahead of me with her shoes on.

A lay nun came along to examine our hair, after we had made our beds.

'I have dandruff. I have dandruff,' I said excitedly, in case she'd mistake it for anything else.

She gave me a tap on the cheek with the comb and told me to be quiet. She looked through my hair. 'I don't know what this great weight of hair is for. Our Lady would hardly approve it,' she said as she passed on to the next girl. My honour was saved. The girl next to me, with the squint and the expensive dressing-gown, had nits. 'Disgraceful,' the nun said as she looked through the thin, mousy hair. I was afraid that bugs might crawl from her pillow to mine at night-time.

Just before nine we went to our classrooms. Baba sat in the desk with me. We sat in the back row. Baba said it was safer back there, and while we were waiting for the nun to come Baba wrote out a little rhyme in her copybook. It was:

The boys sit on the back bench
The girls in front quite still.
The boys are not supposed to pinch
But there are boys who will.

A girl is asked to tell
If a boy pinches from behind.
Some girls yell
But some girls don't mind.

The first nun who came to the classroom was young and very pretty. Her skin was pink-white and almost moist. Like rose petals in the early morning. She taught us Latin and began by teaching us the Latin for table and its various cases. Nominative, vocative, and so on. The lesson lasted forty minutes and then another nun came, who taught us English. There were two new sticks of chalk and a clean suede duster on the table beside her hands. Her hands were very white and she wore a narrow silver ring on one finger. She was twisting the ring round her finger all the time. She was delicate-looking and she read us an essay by G. K. Chesterton.

Then a third nun came to teach us algebra. She began to write on the blackboard and she talked through her nose.

'Nawh, gals,' she said. I wasn't listening. The autumn sun came through the big window and I was looking to see if there were any cobwebs in the corners of the ceilings, as there had been at the National School, when she threw down the chalk and called for every girl's attention. I trembled a little and looked at the x's and y's she had written on the blackboard. The morning dragged on until lunch time. Lunch was terrible.

First there was soup. Thin, grey-green soup. And sections of dry, grey bread on our side-plates.

'It's cabbage water,' Baba said to me. She had changed places with the girl next to me and I was glad of her company. She wasn't supposed to change, and we hoped that it would go unnoticed. After the soup came the plates of dinner. On each plate there was a boiled, peeled potato, some stringy meat, and a mound of roughly chopped cabbage.

'Didn't I tell you it was cabbage water?' Baba said, nudging me. I wasn't interested. My meat was brutal-looking and it had a faint smell as if gone off. I sniffed it again and knew that I couldn't eat it.

'This meat is bad,' I said to Baba.

'We'll dump it,' she said, sensibly.

'How?' I asked.

'Bring it out and toss it into that damn' lake when we're out walking.' She rooted in her pocket and found an old envelope.

I had the meat on my fork and was just going to put it in the envelope when another girl said, 'Don't. She'll ask you where it's gone to so quickly,' so I put just one slice in the envelope and Baba put a slice of hers.

'Sister Margaret searches pockets,' the girl said to us.

'Talk of an angel,' said Baba under her breath, because Sister Margaret had just come into the refectory and was standing at the head of the table surveying the plates. I was cutting my cabbage, and seeing something black in it I lifted some out on to my bread-plate.

'Caithleen Brady, why don't you eat your cabbage?' she asked.

'There's a fly in it, Sister,' I said. It was a slug really but I didn't like to hurt her feelings.

'Eat your cabbage, please.' She stood there while I put forkfuls into my mouth and swallowed it whole. I thought I might be sick. Afterwards she went away and I put the remainder of my meat into Baba's envelope, which she put inside her jumper.

'Do I look sexy?' she asked, because she bulged terribly at one side.

When our plates were empty we passed them up along to the head of the table.

The lay nun carried in a metal tray which she rested on the corner of the table. She handed round dessert dishes of tapioca.

'Jesus, it's like snot,' Baba said in my ear.

'Oh, Baba, don't,' I begged. I felt terrible after that cabbage.

'Did I ever tell you the rhyme Declan knows?'

'No.'

'"Which would you rather: run a mile, suck a boil, or eat a bowl of snot?" Well, which would you?' she asked, impatiently. She was vexed when I hadn't laughed.

'I'd rather die, that's all,' I said. I drank two glasses of water and we came out.

Classes continued until four o'clock, Then we all crowded into the cloakroom, got our coats, and prepared for our walk. It was nice to go out on the street. But we by-passed the main street and went out a side road, in the direction of the lake. As we passed the water's edge, several parcels of meat were pitched in.

'I have done the deed; didst thou not hear the noise?' said one of the senior girls and the lake was full of little ripples as the small parcels sank underneath. The walk was short and we were hungry and lonely as we passed the shops. It was impossible to go into the shops because there was a prefect in charge of us. We walked in twos and once or twice the girl behind me walked on my heel.

'Sorry,' she kept saying. She was that mopey girl who kept passing me the bread the first evening. Her gym frock dipped down under her navy gaberdine coat and she had steelrimmed spectacles.

'A penny for your thoughts,' Baba said to me, but they were worth more. I was thinking of Mr Gentleman.

After the walk we did our home lessons, then we had tea and then rosary. Rosary over we went round the convent walks. Cynthia came with us and the three of us linked. We walked past the gardens, and smelt damp clay

99

and the spicy perfume of the late autumn flowers; then we climbed the hill that led to the playing-fields. It was almost dusk.

'The evenings are getting shorter,' I said fatally. I said it the way Mama would have said it; and the resemblance frightened me, because I did not want to be as doleful as Mama was.

'Tell us everything,' Cynthia said. Cynthia was gay and secretive and full of spirit. 'Have you boy friends?' she asked.

'An old man,' I thought. But it was absurd to think of him as a boy-friend, after all I was not much more than fourteen. Already our day in Limerick seemed far away, like a dream.

'Have *you?*' Baba asked her.

'Oh yeh. He's terrific. He's nineteen and he works in a garage. He has his own motor-bicycle. We go to dances and everything on it,' she said. Her voice was flushed. She liked remembering it.

'Are you fast?' Baba asked bluntly.

'What's fast?' I interrupted. The word puzzled me.

'It's a woman who has a baby quicker than another woman,' Baba said quickly, impatiently.

'Is it, Cynthia?' I asked.

'In a way.' She smiled. Her smile was for the motor-bicycle, riding with a red kerchief round her hair, over a country road with fuchsia hedges on either side; her arms clasped round his waist. Her ear-rings dangling like the fuchsia flowers.

'Tighter, tighter,' he was saying. She obeyed him. Cynthia was not an angel, but very very grown up.

We sat *in a* summer-house up on the hill and watched the

other girls as they trooped past in groups of three or four. There were garden seats piled on top of one another in one corner of the summer-house, and there were a lot of garden tools thrown on the floor.

'Who uses these?' I asked.

'The nuns,' Cynthia said. 'They have no gardener now,' she laughed, slyly to herself.

'Why?' I was curious.

'A nun ran away with the gardener last year. She used to be out here helping him, arranging flower-beds and all that, and didn't they get friendly! So she ran off.' This was excitement, the kind of thing we liked to hear. Baba sat forward and brightened considerably at the prospect of hearing something lively.

'How'd she manage it?' she asked Cynthia.

'At night, over the wall.'

Baba began to hum. 'And when the moon shines, over the cowshed, I'll be waiting at the ki-i-itchen door.'

'Did he marry her?' I asked. I found myself trembling again; trembling with anxiety until I had heard the end of the story; trembling because I wanted it to have a happy ending.

'No. We heard he left her after a few months,' Cynthia said, casually.

'Oh God!' I exclaimed.

'Oh God, my eye! She was no beauty when she climbed over the wall to meet him. Bald and everything. 'Twas all right when she was a nun, she had the white gamp around her face and she looked mysterious. And I imagine that dress she wore was hickish.'

'Whose dress?' Baba asked. Baba was always practical.

'Marie Duffy's. She's the prefect this year. The nun was

101

in charge of the Christmas concert, and Marie Duffy got a dress from home to play Portia in. After the concert the dress was hanging up in the cloakroom; and then one day it disappeared. I suppose the nun took it.'

The convent bells rang out, summoning us away from the summer-house and the smell of clay and the joy of shared secrets. We ran all the way back to the school and Cynthia warned us not to tell.

That night, when I was going to bed, Cynthia kissed me on the landing. She kissed me every night after that. We would have been killed if we were caught.

Baba saw us and she was hurt. She hurried into the dormitory, and when I went to whisper her good night she looked at me with a sort of despondent look.

'All that talk about old Mr Gentleman was a joke,' she said.

She was begging me to exclude Cynthia from our walks and our little chats together. I think I stopped being afraid of Baba that night, and I went to bed quite happily.

The girl whose bed backed on to mine was munching under the covers. I could hear her. For a long time I expected something from her, because I'd brought my seed cake over to the refectory and divided it out amongst the whole table. I didn't do this to be generous; I did it because I was afraid. Afraid of being caught and afraid of drawing mice into my press. Hickey said that girls who were afraid of mice were afraid of men too.

She was eating for hours. In the end I got desperate. I was going to ask her for a bit, but finally I remembered the Vick vapour-rub in my toilet-bag. I often tasted it at home and I knew that it had a sickening taste. So I reached out, got it from under my wash-stand, and put a small blob on the back of my tongue. It killed the hunger at once.

I went to sleep wondering if I should write to him; and wondering if Mrs Gentleman read his letters.

10

The days passed. Days made different only by the fact that it was raining outside; or the leaves were falling; or our algebra nun got a new crocheted shawl. Her old black one was gone green and had frayed at the edges. She was proud of the new one, and whenever she took it off she shook the rain out of it, and spread it carefully over the radiator. The central heating was on, but the radiators were only faintly warm. In between classes we warmed our hands on the one that was close to our desk. Baba said we'd get chilblains and we did.

Baba had got very quiet and she was not a favourite with the nuns. She was put standing for three hours in the chapel, because Sister Margaret overheard her saying the Holy Name. She was stupid at lessons although she was so smart in her conversation otherwise. I came first in the weekly tests and the strain of this nearly killed me. Always worrying in case I shouldn't come first the following week. So I used to study at night in bed with the light of a flash-lamp.

'Jesus, you'll get cross-eyed and it serves you right,' Baba said when she saw me reading a book under the covers, but I told her that I liked studying. It kept my mind off other things.

One Saturday a few weeks later Sister Margaret gave us our letters. She had already opened them.

'Who are these gentlemen?' she asked as she handed me two envelopes; one from Hickey and the other from Jack Holland. There was a third letter, from my father. It was like a letter to a stranger. He said that he had moved to the gate-lodge and was happy there. He added that the big house was too much anyhow, now that Mama had gone. I made a tour in my mind of all the rooms; I saw the patchwork quilts, the home-made crinothine fire-screens edged with red piping, and the damp walls painted with flat green oil-paint. I could even open drawers and see the things Mama had laid into them – old Christmas decorations, empty perfume bottles, silk underwear in case she ever had to go to hospital; spare sets of curtains, and everywhere white balls of camphor.

Bull's-Eye misses you, and so do I. With these words he concluded the short letter and I crumpled it up in my hand because I didn't want to read it again.

Jack Holland's note was as flowery as I had expected. His handwriting was spidery and he wrote on ruled copybook pages. He talked of the clemency of the weather and two lines later he said he was taking precautions against the downpours. Which meant that he was putting basins in the upstairs rooms to catch the water and if there were not enough basins he would put old dishcloths there to soak up the drips from the ceilings. One paragraph of his letter puzzled me. It read:

And, my dear Caithleen, who is the image and continuation of her mother, I see no reason why you shall not return and inherit your mother's home and carry on her admirable domestic tradition.

I wondered if he was going to give the place back to me; but another thought flitted across my mind and I laughed to myself. He said that himself and his invalid mother were not living in our house but that he had an attractive offer from an order of nuns who wished to rent it as a novitiate. French nuns, he said. Nice for Mr Gentleman, I thought, acidly. *He* hadn't written and I was disappointed.

A photograph fell out of Hickey's letter, a passport photograph of himself that he had got taken for his journey to England. There he was, beaming and happy and very self-conscious; exactly like himself, except that he had a collar and tie on in the picture, whereas at home he wore his shirt open and you could see the short black hairs on his chest. His spelling was all wrong. He said Birmingham was sooty, with *droves of people everywhere and porter twice the price.* He had a job as a night watchman in a factory, so he was able to sleep all day. He sent me a postal order for five shillings and I thanked him several times over, hoping that if I said it often enough he would divine it over there in black Birmingham. I kept it for the Halloween party.

October dragged on. The leaves fell and there were piles of leaves under the trees; piles of brown, withered leaves that had curled up at the edges. Then one day a man came and gathered them into a heap and made a bonfire in the corner of the front garden. That night when we were going up to the rosary, the fire was still smoking and the grounds had the wistful smell of leaf smoke. After the rosary we talked about the Halloween party.

'Get the one with the nits,' Baba said to me. She meant the girl in the bed next to mine.

'Why?' I knew Baba hated her.

106

'Because her damn' mother has a shop and the reception-room is bursting with parcels for her.' The parcels for the Halloween party were coming every day. I couldn't ask my father for one because a man is not able to do these things; so I wrote to him for money instead and a day-girl bought me a barm-brack, apples, and monkey-nuts.

When the day came for the party we carried small tables from the convent down to the recreation hall; we sat in groups of five or six and shared the contents of our parcels. Cynthia and Baba and the girl with the nits, whose name was Una, and myself shared the same table. Una got four boxes of chocolates and three shop cakes and heaps of sweets and nuts.

'Have a sweet, Cynthia?' Baba said, opening Una's chocolates; but Una didn't mind. No one liked her and she was always bribing people to be her friend. Cynthia got lovely home-made oatcakes and when you ate them the coarse grains of oats stuck in your teeth.

'Have one, Sister,' Cynthia said to Sister Margaret who was walking in and out among the tables. She was smiling that day. She even smiled at Baba. She took two oatcakes but she didn't eat them. She put them into her side pocket and when she moved away Baba said, 'They starve themselves.' I think she was right.

'You got a hell of a stingy parcel,' Baba noted, leaning over to look into the cardboard box of mine that had the barm-brack and the few things in it. I blushed and Cynthia squeezed my hand under the table. Baba had mixed her own things with Una's, so that I wasn't sure what she had got. But I know that Martha told her to share with me. We ate until we were full, and afterwards we cleared off the tables and the floor was littered with nutshells, apple-cores, and toffee-papers. Nearly every girl was wearing a barm-brack ring. Then we went up to the chapel to pray for the Holy Souls and Cynthia had her arm round my waist.

'Don't mind Baba,' she said to me tenderly. But I had minded. Baba walked behind with Una. Una gave her an unopened box of chocolates and some tangerines. The tangerine skin had an exotic smell and I brought some in my pocket so that I could smell it in the chapel.

'See you tonight,' Cynthia said. We put on our berets and went in. The chapel was almost dark, except for the light from the sanctuary lamp up near the altar. We prayed for the souls in Purgatory. I thought of Mama and cried for a while. I put my face in my hands so that the girls next to me would think I was praying or meditating or something. I was trying to recall how many sins she had committed from the time she was at Confession to the time she died. I knew that we had been given too much change in one of the shops and I said I'd bring it back.

'You will not, they have more than that out of us,' she said, and she put the change into the cracked jug on the pantry shelf. And she had told a lie too. Mrs Stevens from the cottages came up to borrow the donkey and Mama said the donkey was in the bog with Hickey; when all the time the donkey was above in the kitchen garden asleep under the pear tree with his knees bent. I saw him there because Mama had sent me to look for the black hen who was laying out. Every year the black hen laid out and hatched her chickens in the ditch. It was a miracle to see her wander back to the hen-house with a clutch of lovely little furry yellow chickens behind her. When I had stopped crying my face was red and my eyelids hot.

'What are you dripping about?' Baba asked me when we came out.

'Purgatory,' I said.

'Purgatory. What about hell, burning for ever and ever?' I could see flames and I could smell clothes scorching.

'You'd never guess who wrote to me,' she said. Her voice was perky and she had a mint in her mouth.

'Who?' I asked.

'Old Mr Gentleman.' She turned towards me as she said it.

'Show it to me,' I said anxiously.

'What in the hell do you take me for?' she said and she went on ahead, skipping lightly in her black patent leather shoes.

'I'll ask him at Christmas,' I called after her, but Christmas seemed years away.

And yet it came.

One day in the middle of December we prepared for the holidays. Cynthia gave me a hanky satchet for a present and I was awarded a statue of St Jude for coming first place in the Christmas examination. We looked out through the window all evening, expecting Mr Brennan's car. He came just after six o'clock, and we put on our coats and followed him out to the car. The three of us sat in front and Mr Brennan lit himself a cigarette before we set off. The cigarette smelt lovely and it was nice to sit there while he started the car and turned on lights and then drove slowly down the avenue. Soon we were out of the town and driving between the stone walls that skirted the road on both sides. The darkness was delicious. We could almost smell it. We talked all the time and I talked more than Baba. There were milk tanks on wooden stands outside the farm gates that we drove past.

A rabbit ran out from the wall and darted across the road in the glare of the headlights.

'Got 'im,' Mr Brennan said as he slowed down. He got out and walked back forty or fifty yards. He left the door open and the cold air came into the car. It was nice to feel the cold air. The convent was prison. He flung the rabbit on the back seat. It was stretched out along the length of the black leather seat. I couldn't see it in the dark, but I knew how it looked and I knew there was blood somewhere on its soft, dun-coloured fur.

When we stepped out of the car outside Brennans' there were lights in all the front windows and there was excitement behind the lights. We ran in ahead of Mr Brennan and Martha kissed us in the hall. Molly and Declan kissed us too and we went into the drawing-room. My father sat in front of the big blazing fire with his feet inside the oak kerb.

'Welcome home,' he said and he stood up and kissed us both. The room was warm and happy. The curtains were different. They were red hand-woven ones and there were cushions to match on the leather armchairs. The table was set for tea, and I could smell the delicious smell of hot mince-pies. A spark flew out on to the sheepskin rug and Martha rushed across to step on it. She wore a black dress and I hated to admit to myself that she had got older. Somehow in the few months she had passed over into middle-age and her face was not quite so defiantly beautiful.

'Marvellous fire,' I said, warming my hands and enjoying the smell of the turf.

'I provide that,' my father said proudly. At once, I felt the old antagonism which I had towards him.

'I keep them supplied in turf and timber,' he said a second time. I thought of saying 'How in God's name can you do that, when you don't own a cabbage garden?' but it was my first night home and I said nothing. Anyhow, I supposed that he had kept some turf banks and perhaps a wood or two at the very far boundary where the farm degenerated in wild birch woods.

'You got tall,' he said to me ominously, as if it were abnormal for a girl of fourteen to grow.

'Tomorrow's dinner, Mammy,' Mr Brennan said as he carried in the slaughter. He had it held by the two hind legs and it was a very long rabbit.

'Oh no,' Martha said wearily, and she put her hand across her eyes.

'That man has never gone out but he's brought something back for tomorrow's dinner,' she said to my father, when Mr Brennan went down to the scullery to wash his hands and to hang the rabbit in the meat-safe.

'A, good complaint,' my father replied. He had no insight into the small irritations that could drive people mad.

Before supper we went upstairs to change our clothes. Molly carried the brass candlestick and Martha called after her not to spill grease all over the stair-carpet. The thought of getting into a coloured dress and silk stockings after months of black clothes raised my heart. I felt sorry for the poor nuns, who never changed at all. Molly had our clothes airing in the hot press and she carried them into the bedroom.

'That's yours,' she said, pointing to a parcel on the bed. I opened it and found a pair of brown, high-heeled, suede shoes. I put them on and walked unsteadily across the floor, for Molly's approval.

'They're massive,' she said. They were. Nothing I had ever got before gave me such immense pleasure. I looked in the wardrobe mirror at myself and admired my legs a thousand times. My calves had got fatter and my legs were nicely shaped. I was grown up.

'Where did they come from?' I said at last. In the excitement I had forgotten to ask.

'Your dad got them for you, for Christmas,' she said. She liked my father and gave him a cup of tea every time he called to the house. A twinge of guilt overtook me and lowered my spirits for a second. I found it difficult to come downstairs and thank him. And even when I did thank him, he had no idea that the shoes gave me such secret pleasure. All through supper I was lifting up the big white tablecloth to look at my feet under the table. Finally I sat sideways, so that I could look at them constantly and admire my legs in the golden nylon stockings. The stockings were a present from Martha.

We had ham and pickles for supper, and home-made fruit cake that Martha had made specially for us.

''Tis reeking with nutmeg,' Baba said. Cooking was her best subject at school. She looked pretty in her white overall rolling pastry, and her face was always coyly flushed as she stood near the oven waiting to take out an apple-pie or to test a madeira cake with a knitting-needle.

'How much nutmeg d'you use?' Baba asked her mother.

'Just a ball,' said Martha innocently; and Baba laughed so much that the crumbs went down her windpipe and we had to thump her on the back. Declan ran off for a glass of water. She drank some and finally she was calm again. Declan was wearing long grey-flannel trousers and Baba said that his bottom looked like two eggs tied in a handkerchief. He was trying to catch my eye, all the time through supper, and he was winking at me furiously.

The door-bell rang, and after a second Molly tapped on the drawing-room door and said: 'Mr Gentleman, Mam. He's come to see the girls.'

When he walked into the room I knew that I loved him more than life itself.

'Good night, Mr Gentleman,' we all said. Baba was nearest the door and he kissed the top of her head and patted her hair for a minute. Then he came round the side of the table and my knees began to quake at the prospect of his kissing me.

'Caithleen,' he said. He kissed me on the lips. A quick dry kiss, and he shook hands with me. He was shy and strangely nervous. But when I looked into his eyes they were saying the sweet things which they had said before.

'No kiss for me?' Martha said, as she stood behind him with a tumbler of whiskey in her hand. He gave her a kiss on the cheek and took the whiskey. Mr Brennan said that as it was Christmas time he'd have a drink himself and we all sat round the fire.' I wanted to clear off the table but Martha said to leave it. My father filled himself several cups of cold tea from the tea-pot and Baba went off with Martha to put hot-water bottles in our bed. Mr Gentleman and Mr Brennan were talking about foot-and-mouth disease. My father coughed a little to let them know that he was there; and he passed them cigarettes two or three times but they did not include him in the conversation because he was in the habit of saying stupid things. Finally, he played Ludo with Declan and I was sorry for him.

I just sat there on the high-backed chair, admiring the colours in the turf flames. Every few seconds Mr Gentleman gave me a look that was at once sly and loving and full of promises. When at last he noticed my new shoes and my legs flattered in the new nylons his eyes dwelt on them for a while as if he were planning something in his mind, and he took a long drink of whiskey and said it was time to go.

'See you tomorrow,' he said directly to me.

'Are you going my way, sir?' my father asked him; knowing that of course he was. He offered my father a seat in the car and they both left.

'Well, it's lovely to see you here again,' Mr Brennan said, as he put his arms round me. He was always a little maudlin after a few drinks. He was sleepy too and his eyes kept closing.

'You should go to bed,' Martha said to him. He opened the buttons of his waistcoat and said good night to all of us and went off to bed.

'Go to bed, Declan,' Martha said.

'Ah, Mammy,' he pleaded. But Martha insisted. When they were gone she filled three glasses of sherry and gave us a glass each. We sat, huddled in over the fire, and talked, the way women who like each other can talk; once the men are out of sight.

'How's life?' Baba said.

'Lousy,' Martha said, and she told us all that had happened since we went away. The fire had died into a bed of grey ashes before we climbed the stairs. Martha carried the lamp and its light was very dim, because the oil was nearly burnt out. She put it in the hallway between our room and hers, and when we had undressed she came out and quenched it. Mr Brennan was snoring, and she went to her own room, sighing.

11

Next day was cold. Mr Gentleman called for me after lunch. Baba had gone up the street to show off her new mohair coat, and Martha was lying down. Baba told me in great secrecy that Martha was going through the change of life; and I sympathized with her. I didn't know what it meant; except that it had something to do with not having babies.

Molly was brushing the collar of my coat in the hall when the door-bell rang.

'You wanted a seat to Limerick,' Mr Gentleman said. He was wearing a black nap-coat and his face looked petrified.

'I did,' I said, and kicked Molly's toe with my shoe. Earlier I had told her that I was going out to visit my mother's sister, and that he was giving me a lift.

We said nothing for a long time after I got into the car. It was a new car with red-leather seats and the ashtray was stuffed with cigarette-ends. I wondered whose they were.

'You got plump,' he said finally. I hated the sound of the word. It reminded me of young chickens when they were being weighed for the market.

'You got pretty too – terribly pretty,' he said, frowning. I thanked him and asked him how his wife was. Such a stupid question! I could have killed myself.

'She's well, and how are you? Have you changed?' There were all sorts of meanings behind his words and behind the yellow-grey lustre of his eyes. Even though his face was weary, life-weary, and dead in a peculiar way, his eyes were young and large and fiercely expectant.

'Yes, I have changed. I know Latin and algebra. And I can do square roots.' He laughed and told me that I was funny; and we drove away from the gate, because Molly was looking out the sitting-room window at us. She had a corner of the lace curtain lifted, and her nose flat against the window-pane.

I closed my eyes as we passed our own gate. I had no wish to see it.

'Can I hold your hand?' he asked, gently. His hand was freezing and his nails were almost purple with the cold. We drove along the Limerick road and while we were driving it began to snow. Softly the flakes fell. Softly and obliquely against the windscreen. It fell on the hedges and on the trees behind the hedges, and on the treeless fields in the distance, and slowly and quietly it changed the colour and the shape of things, until everything outside the motorcar had a mantle of white soft down.

'There's a rug in the back of the car,' he said. It was a tartan wool rug and I would have liked to wrap it round us but I was too shy. I watched the snow-flakes tumble through the air. The car was slowing down and I knew that before the flakes began to show on the front bonnet Mr Gentleman was going to say that he loved me.

True enough he drove down a side track and stopped the car. He cupped my face between his cold hands and very solemnly and very sadly he said what I had expected him to say. And that moment was wholly and totally perfect for me;

and everything that I had suffered up to then was comforted in the softness of his soft, lisping voice; whispering, whispering, like the snow-flakes. A hawthorn tree in front of us was coated white as sugar, and the snow got worse and was blowing so hard that we could barely see. He kissed me. It was a real kiss. It affected my entire body. My toes, though they were numb and pinched in the new shoes, responded to that kiss, and for a few minutes my soul was lost. Then I felt a drip on the end of my nose and it bothered me.

'Blue Noses,' I said, looking for my handkerchief.

'What are blue noses?' he asked.

'The title for winter noses,' I said. I had no handkerchief so he loaned me his.

On the way back he had to get out a few times because the windscreen-wipers got choked up. Even for the second he was away I was lonesome for him.

I was home in time for tea and we had boiled eggs. Mine was fresh and boiled to the right hardness and I had forgotten its lovely country flavour. Eating it, I thought of Hickey, and I decided to post him a dozen of fresh eggs to Birmingham.

'Can you post eggs to England?' I asked Baba. There was egg yolk all over her lips and she was licking it.

'Can you post eggs to England? Of course you can post eggs to England if you want the postman to deliver a box of sop and mush with egg white running up his sleeve. If you want to be a moron you can post eggs to England but they'll turn into chickens on the way.'

'I only asked,' I said, peevishly.

'You're a right-looking eejit,' she said. She was making faces at me. There were only the two of us at the table.

'What are you sending Cynthia for Christmas?' I asked.

'I won't tell you. Mind your own bloody business.'

'I won't tell *you*,' I said.

'As a matter of fact I have given her mine. A valuable piece of jewellery,' Baba told me.

'Not the ring I gave you?' I asked. It was the only piece of jewellery she had brought with her to the convent. We weren't allowed to wear trinkets there, so she kept the ring in her rosary-bead purse. I finished my tea quickly and went out to the hall and searched in her pocket for the purse. The ring was gone out of it. Mama's favourite ring. Once Baba had got something, she no longer valued it.

I put on my coat and went upstairs for my flash-lamp. There was a light showing under Martha's door so I knocked and stuck my head in. She was sitting up in bed with a cardigan over her shoulders.

'I'm going up the street. I won't be long,' I said.

'Don't. We're playing cards tonight, all of us. Your dad is coming over.' She smiled faintly. She was suffering. She was paying back for all the gay nights that she'd spent down at the hotel, her legs crossed, her tongue tasting a thick, expensive liqueur. She and Mr Brennan slept in separate beds.

The snow had turned to slush in the few hours and the footpath was slippy. The battery of my lamp was almost gone and the light kept fading. It was hard to see and I wasn't used to the darkness. Still, I remembered where the steps were, just before the hotel, and two more steps before I crossed the bridge. The water had the same urgent sound and I thought of the day Jack Holland and myself leaned over the stone bridge and looked for fish down underneath. I was on my way to see him, just then.

Water ran down the street too in the dykes where the snow had melted. It was bitterly cold.

There had been a turkey market that day and there were a lot of horses and carts outside the shops. The horses were neighing and jerking their heads to keep themselves warm and you could almost see their breaths turning into plumes of frost. The windows of the drapery shops were dressed for Christmas with holly and Christmas stockings and shreds of tinsel. I couldn't see them very well with my flash-lamp but inside in the shops there were countrywomen buying boots and vests and calico. I looked in the doorway of O'Brien's drapery and saw Mrs O'Brien, under the lamplight, measuring curtain material. There was a countryman sitting on a chair fitting on a pair of boots, and his wife was feeling the leather with her hands and searching to see if his toe came to the very tip of the boot. Jack's shop was next door. I went in, hoping there would be lots of people drinking in the bar. Alas, it was empty. Jack sat like a ghost behind the counter, writing into a ledger with the light of a very dim handlamp.

'Dearest,' he said, when he looked up and saw me. He took off his steel-rimmed glasses and came outside to greet me. He brought me in behind the counter and sat me on a tea-chest. There was an oil-stove at my feet and it was smoking. The shop smelt of paraffin oil.

'An Irish colleen,' he said, and sneezed fiercely. He took out an old flannel rag and while he was blowing his nose I looked at the ledger that he had been writing in. There was a dead moth on the opened page and a brown stain just below it. When he saw that I was looking at it, he closed the book, being very secretive about his customers.

'Who's there? Who is it, Jack?' a voice called from the kitchen.

It was exactly the voice one would expect from an old, dead woman. It was high and hoarse and croaking.

'Jack, I'm dying. I'm dying,' the voice moaned. I jumped off the tea-chest but Jack put a hand on my shoulder and made me sit down again.

'She's just curious to know who's here,' he said. He didn't bother to whisper.

'It's thrilling to see you,' he said, beaming at me. The beam divided his lips and I saw his last three teeth. They were like brown, crooked nails and I imagined that they were loose.

'Thrilling,' I said to myself, and wondered if he thought Goldsmith thrilling.

'Jack, I'm dying,' the voice said again; and Jack swore bad-temperedly and ran into the kitchen. I followed him.

'Good God Almighty, you're on fire,' he shouted. There was a smell of something burning.

'On fire,' she said, looking at him like a baby.

'Goddamn it, take your shoe out of the ashes,' he said. She had the toe of her black canvas shoe in the bed of ashes under the grate.

She was an old bent woman dressed in black; a little black shadow doubled up in a rocking-chair. The fire had died into grey clinkers that were still red in the centre and the ashes hadn't been cleaned out for a week. The kitchen was big and draughty.

'A sup o' milk,' she said. I was sure she was dying. Her eyes had that desperate, dying look. I looked in the jugs along the table for milk. There was some in the bottom of two jugs, but it had gone sour.

'Over there,' Jack said, pointing to a fresh can of milk on the form along the wall. He was holding her by the shoulders because she had taken a fit of coughing. There were hens on the form picking out of a colander of cold cabbage and when I went near them they flew down and crossed over to the bottom step of the stairs. The milk was fresh and yellow and there were specks of dust floating on the top of it.

'It's dusty,' I said.

'There's a cheesecloth on the dresser,' he pointed. I strained some of the milk through the yellowed, smelly strip of dried muslin and he put the cup to her lips.

'I don't want it,' she said and I could have shaken her. After all that commotion she said she wanted a sweet.

'A sweet for the cough,' she said, gasping for breath between the words. He took some sugar-coated pastilles out of the salt-hole in the wall and wiped the dust off them. He put two between her lips and she sucked them like a child. Then she looked at me and beckoned for me to come over.

A candle stood on the mantelpiece beside her and though it had nearly burnt out the wick had sprung into a final, tall flame, and I could see her face very clearly. The yellow skin stretched like parchment over her old bones and her hands and her wrists were thin and brown like boiled chicken bones. Her knuckles were bent with rheumatism, her eyes almost dead, and I hated to look at her. I was looking at death.

'I must go, Jack,' I said suddenly. I was suffocating.

'Not yet, Caithleen,' he said, and he eased her back in the chair. He put a cushion at the back of her head so that the hard chair did not hurt her scalp. Her hair was white and thin like an infant's. She smiled as I walked away.

Out in the shop Jack filled me a glass of raspberry cordial and I wished him a happy Christmas.

'Thank you for your letters,' I said.

'You have caught their full implication?' he said, raising his eyes so that his forehead broke into worried lines.

'What implication?' I asked, foolishly. So very foolishly.

'Caithleen,' he said, as he breathed deeply and caught hold of my hands. 'Caithleen, in time to come I hope to marry you,' and the red cordial in my throat froze to ice.

I got away somehow. There was a threat that the chapped, colourless lips would endeavour to kiss mine, so I put the glass on the counter and said, 'My father is waiting outside, Jack, I'll have to run.' I ran and the little latch that clicked as I closed the door clicked on Jack's face that was transformed with a vague, happy smile. I suppose he thought that he had made a success of it.

I fell over a damn' dog in the outside porch. He yelped and turned round as if he were going to bite me, but in the end he didn't.

'Happy Christmas,' I said to him in gratitude, and went down the street. A motor-car drove up the hill towards me. The headlights were blinding. It slowed down as it came to the top of the hill. It was Mr Gentleman's.

'Are you going somewhere?' I asked.

'Yes, I came over for petrol,' he said. It was a lie. I sat in beside him and he warmed my fingers. I put my gloves in my coat pocket.

'Will we go in to Limerick for dinner?' he asked. His voice was very tentative as if he expected to be refused.

'I can't. I'm going home to play cards. I promised them, and my father is coming over.' He sighed, but otherwise he was quite resigned. It was then that he noticed that I was shivering.

'Caithleen, what's wrong?' he asked. I tried to tell him about Jack and the old woman's shoe smouldering away, and the sour milk, and the candle dying in the dirty saucer, and the smell of must on everything. And I told him also about Jack's proposal and how idiotic it was.

'Curious,' he said, as he smiled.

'Please have more feeling, Mr Gentleman,' I begged of him in my mind.

'Have to go now,' he said and we turned the car in the alley of the bakery shop. I was lonely with him then, because he had not understood what I had been telling him.

He dropped me at the gate and said that he was going home to bed.

'So early?' I asked.

'Yes, I didn't sleep last night, only on and off.'

'Why not?'

'You know why.' His voice caressed me and his eyes were almost crying when I got out and shut the door gently. He had to open it again and give it a proper bang.

When I went into the hall I knew there was something wrong. Molly and Martha had decorated the Christmas tree and it was standing in a red wooden bucket at the side of the hall-stand. It was pretty, with icicles trembling on it and orange sugar-barleyed candles rising out of the green needles. But something *was* wrong.

'Caithleen,' Martha called me into the room.

'Caithleen,' she said, fatally, 'your daddy hasn't come.'

'Why?' I asked, not thinking of the old reason.

'He's gone, Caithleen – off on a batter. He was giving away flyers in an hotel in Limerick a half an hour ago.' I sat down on the arm of her chair and played with the button of my coat and felt the happiness drain out of me.

Molly stopped blowing balloons for a second to tell me something.

'He came here looking for you in the evening, and he said 'twas a wonder you didn't go over to see your father instead of off driving with big-shots,' Molly said, calmly. Mr Gentleman was a big-shot because he never drank in the local pubs, and because he had visitors from Dublin and foreign places. They came to stay with him in the summer. Once a Chief Justice from New York had come and it was mentioned in the local paper.

Baba had the pack of cards in her hands and she was juggling them idly. We played, as we had arranged, and they were all very nice to me and Baba let me win even though I was a fool at cards. Afterwards Molly carried the tree in and put it beside the piano. Some of the icicles fell off and she had to pick them up again.

That Christmas, then, like all the others, was one of waiting, waiting for the worst, except that I was safe in the Brennans' house. But of course I was never safe in my thoughts, because when I thought of things I was afraid. So I visited people every day, and not once did I go over the road to look at our own house. Declan told me that there were shutters on the windows and I wondered what the foxes thought when they went into the empty hen-houses. Bull's-Eye came most days for food and he cried and moaned the first day when he saw me, and smelt my clothes.

Late on Christmas Eve Mr Gentleman came when all the others were out. Molly had gone to get a seat in the chapel, two hours before the midnight Mass; and the Brennans went to Limerick to get wine and last-minute things for the

Christmas dinner. The turkey was stuffed and there were several boxes wrapped in fancy paper laid under the tree. A lot of the pine needles had dropped on to the fawn carpet and I was picking them up when he rang. I guessed that it was him. He came in and kissed me in the hall and gave me a little package. It was a small gold watch with a bracelet of gold lace.

'It ticks,' I said, putting it to my ear. It was so small that I had expected it to be a toy. He was going to kiss me again but we heard a car and he drew back from me, guiltily.

'Oh, Caithleen, we'll have to be very careful,' he said. The car went past the gate.

'It's not them,' I said and went closer to thank him for the beautiful present.

'I love you,' he whispered.

'I love you,' I said. I wished that there was some other way of saying it, some more original way.

My neck was hurting the way he had me held, but it was nice, despite that. I knew the smell of his skin by then and the strength of his arms, shielding me.

'We'll have to be very careful,' he said a second time.

'We are,' I replied. I hadn't seen him for two days and thought it a lifetime.

'I can't see you too often. It's difficult,' he said. He stammered over the last word. He hated to say it. I shook my head. I, too, was sorry for that tall, dark woman who lived so entirely to herself behind the trees and the white stone house. No one ever saw her except to get a glimpse of her when she knelt in the back seat of the chapel on Sundays. She always hurried away before the last gospel and drove off in Mr Gentleman's car. I admired her strength, and it puzzled me why she never bothered to make herself handsome. Always in tweed things and flat laced shoes and mannish hats with a wide brim on them.

'Can I write to you?' I asked. He had kissed me behind the ear, in a place that made me shudder.

'No,' he said, firmly.

'And will I ever see you?' I asked. My voice was more tragic than I meant it to be.

'Of course,' he said, impatiently. It was the first time he looked irritated and I winced. He was sorry at once.

'Of course, of course, my little darling; later, when you go to Dublin.' He was stroking my hair and his eyes looked far ahead and longingly towards the future.

Then he pushed up my sleeve and put the watch on my wrist and we went in and sat at the fire until we heard the car coming. I sat on his lap and he opened his overcoat and let the sides of it drop on to the floor.

'Where will I say I got the watch?' I asked as I jumped up. The car was coming in the front drive.

'You won't say. You'll put it away,' he said.

'But I can't, that's cruel.'

'Caithleen, go up and put it somewhere,' he told me. He lit himself a cigar and tried to look casual as he heard the front door being opened. Baba rushed in with her arms full of parcels.

'Hello, Baba, I came to wish you happy Christmas,' he said, lying, as he took some of the parcels out of her arms and laid them on the hall table.

I put the watch into a china soap-dish. It curled up very nicely in the bottom of the soap-dish, and it looked as if it were going to sleep. It was a pale gold, the colour of moth dust.

When I came down to the room Mr Gentleman was

talking to Mr Brennan and for the rest of the night he ignored me. Baba held a sprig of mistletoe over his head and he kissed her, and then Martha put the gramophone on and played 'Silent Night', and I thought of the evening when the snow fell on the windscreen and when he parked the car under the hawthorn tree. And I tried to catch his eye but he did not look at me until he was leaving, and then it was a sad look.

And so, of course, the time came for us to go back, and once more we got out our gym frocks and our black cotton stockings.

'I should have cleaned my gym frock,' I said to Baba. 'It's all stained.'

She was looking out at the vegetable garden and she was crying. It was that time of year when the garden was lifeless. The sad, upturned damp clay looked desolate and there was nothing to suggest that things would grow there ever again. Over in the corner there was a hydrangea bush, and the withered flowers looked like old floor-mops. Near it was the rubbish heap, where Molly had just thrown empty bottles and the Christmas tree. It was raining and blowing outside and the sky was dark.

'We'll run away,' she said.

'When? Now?'

'Now! No. From the damn' convent.'

'They'll kill us.'

'They won't find us. We'll go with a travelling show company and be actors. I can sing and act; and you can take the tickets.'

'I want to act, too,' I said, defensively.

'All right. We'll put in an advertisement. "Two female amateurs, one can sing; both have secondary education."'

'But we're not females, we're girls.'

'We could pass as females.'

'I doubt it.'

'Oh Christ, don't damp my spirits. I'll kill myself if I have to stay five years in that gaol.'

'It's not so bad.' I was trying to cheer her.

'It's not so bad for you, winning statues and playing up to nuns. You give me the sick anyhow, jumping up to open and close the damn' door for nuns as if they had cerebral palsy and couldn't do it themselves.' It was true, I did play up to the nuns and I hated her for noticing it.

'All right then, *you* run away,' I said.

'Oh no,' she said, desperately, catching my wrist, 'we'll go together.' I nodded. It was nice to know that she needed me.

She remembered then that she had to get something downstairs and she bolted off.

'Where are you going?'

'To feck a few samples from the surgery.'

I got into my gym frock. It was creased all over and the box pleats had come out at the edges. She came back with a new roll of cotton wool and several little sample tubes of ointments. I picked one tube up off the bed, where she threw them. Its name was printed on a white label and a note underneath which read *For udder infusion.*

'What's this for?' I asked. I was thinking of Hickey milking the fawn cow and holding the teat so that the milk zig-zagged all over the cobbled floor. He did this to be funny, whenever I went up to the cow-house to call him to his tea.

'What's this for?' I asked again.

'Make us look females,' she said. 'We'll rub it into our bubs and they'll swell out; it says it's for udders.'

'We might get all hairy or something,' I said. I meant it.

I distrusted ointments with big names on the label and anyhow it *was* for cows.

'You're a right-looking eejit,' she said. She yelled with laughter.

'Supposing we told your father?' I suggested. I didn't really want to run away.

'Tell my father! He has no bloody feelings. He'd tell us to exercise control. Martha told him the other day that she had an ulcer on her foot and he told her to will it away with the power of the mind. He's a lunatic,' she said. Her eyes were flashing with anger.

'There's no other way so,' I said, flatly.

'We can always get expelled,' she said, carefully measuring each word. And she began to consider the various ways we could achieve that.

12

O n and off, for three years, she thought about it. But I discouraged her by reminding her that we were too young to go to the city. During those three years nothing special happened to us, so I can pass quickly over them.

We did examinations and Baba failed hers. Cynthia left the convent; we cried saying good-bye, and swore lifelong friendship. But after a few months we stopped writing letters. I forget who stopped first.

The holidays were always enjoyable. In the summer Mr Gentleman took me out in his boat. We rowed to an island far out from the shore, and boiled a kettle on his primus stove to make tea. It was a happy time and he often kissed my hand and said I was his freckle-faced daughter.

'Are you my father?' I asked wistfully, because it was nice playing make-believe with Mr Gentleman.

'Yes, I'm your father,' he said as he kissed the length of my arm, and he promised that when I went to Dublin later on he would be a very attentive father. Martha and Baba and everyone thought he was bringing me to see my Aunt Molly. One day, we actually did call. Aunt Molly got very excited at having Mr Gentleman as a guest, and she fussed about and brought down the good cups from the parlour. The cups were dusty and she insisted on putting cream in

Mr Gentleman's tea, though he told her that he used no milk. The cream was a great luxury and she thought she was doing us a favour.

But, all the time, Baba was thinking of how we might escape from the convent. She read film magazines in bed and said we could get into pictures, if we knew anyone in America.

The chance came in March 1952. I mean the chance to escape. We had a retreat in the convent and the priest, who came from Dublin to lecture to us, enjoined us to keep silence in order to think of God and of our souls.

On the second morning of the retreat he told us that the afternoon lecture would be devoted to the sixth Commandment. This was the most important lecture of all and it was also very private. Sister Margaret did not wish that the nuns should come into the chapel while it was going on, as the priest spoke very frankly about boys and sex and things. It was not likely that the nuns would come into the chapel by the main door, but some nun might go into the choir gallery upstairs. To prevent this, Sister Margaret wrote out a warning notice which read *Do not enter – Lecture on here*, and she asked me to pin it on the door upstairs. She chose me because I had rubber-soled shoes and was not likely to go pounding up the convent stairs. I felt nervous and excited as I climbed the oak stairs. It was my first time to go in there, to the nuns' quarters, and I had no idea which door I was to pin the notice on. The stairs were highly polished and the white wall on one side was covered with large paintings. Paintings of the Resurrection, and the Last Supper; and a circular, coloured painting of the Madonna and Child. I hoped that at least I'd see a nun's cell, so that I could tell Baba and the others. We were dying to know what the cells were like, because some senior girl said that the nuns slept on planks, and another girl said that they slept in coffins. On the first landing I paused for breath and dipped my hand in the white marble Holy Water font that curved out from under the windowsill. There was a maidenhair fern trailing out of a Chinese vase and the strands were so long that they dipped on to the pale Indian rug that covered the landing floor.

Slowly I climbed the next flight of steps and saw a wooden door on my right. I decided that this must be it. With four new drawing-pins I secured the notice to the centre panel of the door, and then stood back from it to read it. It was written very clearly and all the letters were even. To the left there was a long, narrow corridor with doors on either side, and though I guessed that these were the cells I did not dare go down and peep through a key-hole. I hurried back to the chapel and was just in time for the beginning of the lecture.

When it was almost over, I nipped out and hurried lip the convent stairs to remove the notice. I found Sister Margaret waiting for me. She was fuming with temper.

'Is this your idea of a joke?' she asked. She opened the door and pointed inwards. It was a lavatory. I had to smile.

'I'm sorry, Sister,' I said.

'You are an evil girl,' she said. Her eyes were piercing me and she was so angry that when she spoke little spits flew out of her mouth and spattered my face.

'I'm sorry, Sister,' I said again. I wondered to myself if the nuns were deprived of the lavatory for the whole evening, and the more I thought of it the funnier it seemed. But I was afraid, too, and shaking like a leaf.

'You have insulted my sisters in religion and you have

vulgarized the name of your school,' she said.

'It was an accident,' I said meekly.

'You will remain standing in front of the Blessed Sacrament for three hours, and you will then apologize to the Reverend Mother.'

After I had stood for the three hours and had apologized to the Reverend Mother I was coming down the convent steps, wiping my eyes with the back of my hand, when Baba accosted me. She held up a sheet of paper and written on it was this: *I have a plan at last that will expel us.*

We were supposed to be on silence so we had to go somewhere to talk. I followed her down to the school and up the back stairs to one of the lavatories.

She began at once – knowing that we couldn't stay in there very long – 'We'll leave a dirty note in the chapel as if it fell out of our prayer-books.' She was shaking all over.

'Oh God, we can't,' I said. I was shaking too – after the Reverend Mother. The scene was in my mind vividly. How I knocked on the door and went into the big, cold parlour. She was sitting on a rostrum, reading her office. She pushed her spectacles farther down her nose, and fixed me with a pair of cold, blue, penetrating eyes.

'So you are the rotten apple,' she said. Her voice was quiet but enormously accusing.

'I'm sorry, Sister,' I said. I should have called her 'Mother', but I was so frightened that I got mixed.

'I'm sorry, Mother,' I repeated.

'Are you?' she asked. The question echoed through the length of the cold room, so that the high, ornamented ceiling seemed to ask 'Are you?' and the gilt clock on the mantelpiece ticked 'Are you?' and everything in that room accused me until I was petrified. It was a comfortless room and I doubted that anyone had ever drunk tea at the great oval table with its thick, strong legs. I was waiting for her to really begin, but she said nothing more and then I realized that the interview was over. I withdrew shamefully, closing the door as quietly as possible behind me, and saw that she was looking after me.

'We can't,' I said to Baba. 'Think of all the trouble.' All I wanted was peace.

'What is it anyhow?' I asked.

'It's this.' She whispered in my ear. Even *she* was a little shy about saying it aloud.

'Oh God.' I put my hand across my mouth, in case I should repeat it.

'There's no "Oh God". There will be hell for three or four days and then we're off. Free.'

'We'll get killed.'

'We won't. Martha won't mind and your aul fella will probably be on a batter, and my aul fella can have a run-an'-jump for himself.'

She took her fountain-pencil out of her pocket and a lovely sky-blue holy picture. It was a picture of the Blessed Virgin coming out of the clouds with a blue cloak opening out behind her.

'You write it,' I said.

'Our two names are going to it,' she said as she knelt down. There on the lavatory seat she wrote it in block capitals. I was ashamed of it then, and I am ashamed of it now. I think it's something you'd rather not hear. Anyhow we both signed our names to it.

Though I closed my eyes and tried not to repeat it, the wicked sentence kept saying itself in my ears, and I was ashamed for Sister Mary, my favourite nun. Because what we wrote concerned her and Father Tom.

Father Tom was the chaplain and Sister Mary was the nun who dressed the altar and served Mass. She was a pretty, pink-checked nun, and she was always smiling as if she had some secret in life that no one else had. Not a smug smile but ecstatic. As Baba wrote it, the door-knob was turned from the outside. Two or three times, impatiently each time.

'Suppose it's her,' I said in a gasping whisper. Baba unlocked the door and went out blushing. Standing there was one of the junior girls. She blessed herself when she saw us and went in hurriedly. God knows what she thought, but the following day when we were disgraced she told everyone that we came out of the lavatory together.

For the remainder of the evening, whenever I saw Sister Margaret come into the study, my legs and knees began to tremble, and I could feel her cruel eyes on me.

So, to avoid her, I went to bed early, because during the retreat we were free to go to bed at any hour before ten o'clock. There was no one in the dormitory when I went up; and it was deathly quiet. I was folding the counterpane when I heard footsteps rushing up the stairs.

'Jesus, Cait, where are you?' Baba called.

'Ssh, ssh,' I said, as Sister Margaret was likely to be snooping about.

'She's gone off to the nut-house,' said Baba. Baba's eyes were flashing and she was so excited, she could hardly talk.

'Is it found?' I asked.

'Found! The whole school knows about it. That mope Peggy Darcy handed it to Sister Margaret below in the recreation hall, and didn't old Margaret think 'twas a prayer and she began to read it, out loud.' I could feel the colour travel up my neck and my hands were perspiring.

'Imagine,' said Baba, 'she read out "Father Tom stuck his long thing", and when she realized what it was she went purple at the mouth and began to fume around the recreation hall. She beat several girls with her strap, and she was yelling, "Where are they, where are they, those children of Satan!"' Baba was enjoying every moment of this.

'Go on,' I begged her.

'She had the holy picture in her hand, and she was beating all before her, so Christ I made a bee-line for the cloakroom and hid in one of the presses. All the girls were yelling by then, though half of the young ones didn't know what the thing meant; so in the end she got so delirious that the prefect had to call another nun, and they carried her off.'

'And what'll we do?' I asked. If only we could run quickly, get out of the place.

'They're looking for us. So for Christ's sake don't tremble or break down or anything. Say 'twas a joke we heard some-where,' Baba warned me, and just then the prefect came into the dormitory and called us out.

As we walked past her she withdrew in close to the wall, because now we were filthy and loathsome; and no one could speak to us. In the hallway girls looked at us as if we had some terrible disease, and even girls who had stolen watches and things gave us a hateful, superior look.

The Reverend Mother was waiting for us in the reception-room. She had a shawl over her shoulders, and her face was deathly pale.

'I wish to say that you must leave here at once,' she said. I tried to apologize, and she addressed me individually.

'Your mind is so despicable that I cannot conceive how you have gone unnoticed all those years. Poor Sister Margaret, she has suffered the greatest shock of her religious life. This afternoon you did a disgusting thing, and now you have done something outrageous,' she said. Her voice was trembling and her poise was gone. She was really upset. I began to cry and Baba gave me a dig in the ribs to shut *up*.

'We can explain,' I said to the Reverend Mother.

'I have already informed your parents, you shall leave tomorrow,' she told us.

That night we were put sleeping in the infirmary, in two separate wards. It was the longest night I have ever lived; and the thought of going home next day was terrifying. All night, a mouse scraped the wainscoting, and I lay awake with my feet curled up under me, thinking of some way that I could put an end to my life.

We left next afternoon and no one said good-bye to us.

'Say the rosary,' Baba said to me, in the back of the hire car. The driver was a stranger but he must have had a great old ride, listening to us, as we prayed and alternated our prayers with surmisal. He was from the convent town and Reverend Mother had hired him. News of our disgrace had gone home ahead of us.

There was a man mowing the Brennans' front lawn when we got out of the car. His name was Charlie and he nodded to us, but he didn't stop the mower. It looked as if 'twas running away from him. It was a cold, sunny day and over under the rhododendron shrub there were crocuses in bloom. Yellow-ochre crocuses. The wind had got inside some of them and the petals had fallen down on the grass. They looked like pieces of crêpe paper, just thrown there. There were primroses too. A cluster of them round the root of the sycamore tree. They cut the tree because they were afraid it would fall on the house in a big wind. Mr Brennan had grown ivy round the root and had trailed it across the ugly brown stump and now there were primroses, merry little primroses, shooting up through the ivy. I had been looking at primrose leaves for seventeen years, and I had never noticed before that their leaves were hairy and old and wrinkled. I kept looking at them. Always on the brink of trouble I look at something, like a tree or a flower or an old shoe, to keep me from palpitating.

'Chrisake, go in,' Baba said. She was walking behind me, dragging the big suitcase across the concrete. She hit the back of my leg with the case and I knocked on the door. Molly let us in. She was a little cold. They must have told her not to be friendly.

Mr Brennan and Martha and my father were in the break-fast-room. I didn't look at any of them directly but I saw that Martha was uneasy. She had a handkerchief in her hand and it was shaking.

'A nice thing. You filthy little –, my father said, coming forward. He was trying to think of a word bad enough to describe me. He had his hand raised, as if he were going to strike me.

'I hate you,' I said, suddenly and vehemently.

"You stinking little foul-mouth,' and he struck me a terrific blow. I fell and hit my head on the edge of the china cabinet and cups rattled inside in it. My cheek was smarting from the blow.

Mr Brennan rushed across the room, and drew up his sleeves.

'Leave her alone,' he said, but my father was about to strike me again.

'Take your hands off her,' Mr Brennan shouted, as he tried to pull my father away. I stood up, and edged over towards Martha.

'I'll do what I like to her,' my father threatened. He was in a raging temper, and I could see him grind his false teeth. He tried to pursue me, but Mr Brennan caught him by the shoulders and led him to the door.

'Get to hell out of here,' he said.

'You can't do this to me,' my father protested.

'Can't I!' said Mr Brennan, as he reached for my father's brown hat and placed it sideways on his head.

'I tell you, you won't get away with this,' my father said, but Mr Brennan chucked him out and banged the door in his face. Out in the hall, we could hear him cursing and swearing, and he beat the door with his fists, because Mr Brennan had turned the key from the inside.

'Go home, Brady,' Mr Brennan said, and within a few seconds we heard him go out the hall door. I was crying, of course, and Martha and Baba were pale and shocked.

The homecoming we had dreaded was over. Instead of it being about us, and the dreadful thing we wrote, it was a scene between Mr Brennan and my father. I knew then that Mr Brennan hated my father, and had always hated him.

'Sit down,' Mr Brennan said to Baba and me. We sat on the couch, and looked imploringly at Martha.

'Mammy, what about some tea?' Mr Brennan said to her, and she smiled vaguely. At least, he was reasonable.

'Hello, I didn't say hello to you,' she said to me as she passed by my chair. She touched the top of Baba's hair tenderly.

'Well, now,' said Mr Brennan, when she had gone out.

'We hated it, we hated it; we love home,' I said to him.

Baba had said nothing since we came into the room. She had her head lowered and her hands clasped, as if she were praying. She was determined not to help.

'We're sorry, we hated it,' I said again, and I repeated:

'We love it here.' He smiled faintly to himself and shook his head. He was touched. Somehow the possibility that we had done this because we were lonely seemed fair and reasonable to him.

'But why didn't you tell me?' he asked, and I was thinking of an answer when the phone rang. He had to go off urgently to the mountains, because there was a sow dying, and we were left to drink the tea and talk to Martha.

Later that evening, I was sitting on the couch in the front room when Mr Brennan came back. He came in to talk to me. It was dusk. We could see the silver gleaming on the sideboard, and there was a smell of hyacinths in the room.

'Declan is doing well at school,' he said. I knew exactly what he was thinking.

'I'm sorry, Mr Brennan. I really am.'

'You know, Caithleen, 'tis a great pity. You were clever at school. You would have gone far. Why did you undermine your whole future?' He held my hand while he was asking me.

'Don't ask me,' I said.

'I know why,' he said. His voice was calm, and his hand was soft and warm. He was a good and gentle man.

'Poor Caithleen, you've always been Baba's tool.'

'I like Baba, Mr Brennan. She's great fun and she doesn't mean any harm.' It was true.

'Ah, if one could only choose one's children,' he said, sadly. A lump came in my throat, and I knew all the things that he was trying to tell me. And it seemed to me that life was a disappointment for him. The years of driving over bad roads at night, crossing fields with the light of a lantern to reach some sick beast in a draughty out-house, had been a waste. Mr Brennan had not found happiness, neither in his wife nor in his children. And the thought came to me that he would have liked Mama as his wife and me as his daughter. I felt that he was thinking so himself.

There was a light knock on the door. He said, 'Come in.' It was my father. Martha must have told him that we were in the sitting-room.

'Good evening.' He spoke cheerfully as if nothing awkward had happened. 'Grand evening.' Mr Brennan clicked on the light. The electricity had come since we were home last time. The friendly lamplight made a shadow on the mantelshelf. It was a white china lamp with a china shade on it. Pure and enchanting, like a child's First Communion veil. It was an old-fashioned oil-lamp that Mr Brennan had adapted for electricity.

'You wouldn't want to mind me. I might shout or anything, but 'tis all over in three minutes,' my father said to both of us, and Mr Brennan said, 'Oh, let's forget it.' I said nothing. Father sat down, and took two pounds out of his coat pocket.

'Here,' he said, throwing them over on to my lap. I thanked him and sat there glumly, while they talked. But the talk was strained, and neither one liked the other any more.

Behind the china lamp there was a postcard. It was a postcard of a dancing girl. A Spanish dancer, in a big red hooped skirt, and a white blouse with fulsome sleeves. I went over and picked it up to look at it. Mr Gentleman's handwriting was on the back, and it said, *Best wishes to all of you.* It had a foreign stamp. I ran out of the room.

'Molly, Molly,' I called. She was upstairs getting ready to go out. She had a boy-friend now.

'Come up,' she answered. I went up and stuck my head in her door. She was bathing her feet in a basin of steaming water.

'I'm crippled with corns,' she said. Her room was small and there was linoleum on the floor.

'Molly, where's Mr Gentleman?' I asked. I couldn't wait and lead up to it casually, though I meant to.

'Off sunning himself,' she said. My heart stopped.

'Why?'

'Mrs Gentleman's nerves are at her; and they're gone off on a cruise to the Mediterranean.' I was vexed and jealous and guilty all at once. But at least it was lucky that he wasn't there to hear of our disgrace. Because he was very polite in his own way and he would have been shocked by our behaviour.

13

I was free to go to another convent because my scholarship was still valid, but Mr Brennan was sending Baba to Dublin to take a commercial course and I said that I would go too. I promised my father that I would do examinations to get into the civil service, but meanwhile I was going to work in a grocery shop.

I answered an advertisement in the paper and got a job as shop assistant with a man named Thomas Burns. Jack Holland gave me a glowing reference which said that I had served my apprenticeship with him. The reference was full of adjectives and flowery talk, and he signed it, *Jack Holland, Author and Spirit Merchant.*

'Of course, Caithleen, if ever you change your mind ... It's a lady's privilege,' he said as he licked the brown business envelope and sealed it by pressing it with his fist.

'Thank you, Jack,' I said. 'I'll think about it.' It was a lie, but it kept him happy. His mother was still dying and the jubilee nurse came two days a week now to attend to her. He went over and opened the wooden drawer of the till. It was stiff and only opened halfway. He stuck his hand far in, to where the notes were kept, and took out a pound, folding it into a small square.

'For your perusal,' he said, stuffing it down inside my

blouse. One of the sharp edges of the square pricked my skin, but I was thankful and I let him shake my hand three or four times in return, and stroke my hair. His stroke was clumsy.

When I came out, I went to O'Brien's drapery and bought some materials for a blouse and a pinafore dress, and went down the street to the dressmaker's. She came to the door with a bunch of plain pins between her teeth and loose white threads all over her dress. 'Come in,' she said. She was about to eat her lunch. The three geraniums on the window-sill were just beginning to flower. Two were vivid red and the other was white. The leaves gave the kitchen a nice greenhouse smell.

'Make them grow,' she said, putting the tea leaves from the breakfast on the geranium plant. She rinsed the tea-pot and made some fresh tea.

'And how do you come to be free, this time of year?' she asked in her buttering-up voice. She lived alone and was the town gossip. She knew when unmarried girls were in trouble, even before they knew it themselves. The priest's housekeeper and herself discussed everything, and every-one, under the sun.

'There's an epidemic in the convent,' I said. Baba and I had agreed on the same story. Not even our parents wanted it known that we were expelled.

'How terrible. Is it a bad one now? And 'tis a wonder that the young Jones one from up the mountain isn't home.'

'No. Mountainy girls don't get this particular epidemic,' I said. She gave me a wicked eye. She was from the mountains herself and cycled there every second Sunday to see her father. She used to bring tins of fruit and a jar of calves-foot jelly in the canvas bag on the back of her bicycle.

'Have this,' she said, handing me a cup of tea and a slice of shop sponge cake. Afterwards she measured me.

'You have a bit of a pot-belly,' she noted. She wanted to get some dig at me. I showed her the postcard, so that she could copy the blouse exactly. She looked at the writing on the back.

'Didn't the Gentlemans go off real sudden,' she said.

'Did they?' I asked. She wrote my measurements in a notebook, and I left soon after. She didn't see me out, which meant that she was vexed with me. She expected me to talk about the Gentlemans. I hoped she wouldn't ruin my two pieces of material out of spite.

It was one of those clear, windy days which we get around that part of the country, with a fine strong wind blowing and clouds sailing happily by. It was clear and windy and airy and I was happy to be alive. The wind was blowing in my face so I pushed my bicycle up the hill. I left it inside the Brennans' gate and walked over the road to see my own home. There were French nuns there now. Only five or six of them, with a mistress of novices in charge of them. Young nuns came from the mother house in Limerick to spend their spiritual year in our large, secluded farmhouse.

The old gateway was abandoned, with nettles growing round it. The nuns had made a new gateway, with concrete piers on either side and concrete walls curving out from the piers. The avenue which had been one of weeds and loose stones and cart tracks was now tarmacked and steam-rolled, and easy to walk on. Some of the trees round the house were cut and the white, weather-beaten hall door was painted a soft kindly green. The curtains of course were different, and Hickey's bee-hive was gone.

'Our Mother is expecting you,' said the little nun who answered the door.

She went off noiselessly down the carpeted hall. The room that was once our breakfast-room seemed utterly strange. I felt that I had never been there before. There was a writing-desk in the corner where the what-not had been, and they had added a mahogany mantelpiece.

'You are welcome,' the Mother said. She was French and she didn't look half as severe as the nuns in the convent. She rang a bell to summon the little nun and asked her to bring some refreshments. I got a glass of milk and a slice of homemade cake that was decorated with blanched almonds. It was difficult, chewing the food while she watched me, and I hoped that I didn't make a noise while I ate.

'And what are you planning to be?' she asked.

'Grocer's apprentice,' I thought of saying but instead I said, 'My father hasn't decided yet.' It sounded pretty impertinent, because Molly had told me that Mother Superior helped my father get over his drinking bouts. She brought down flasks of beef tea when he was in bed, and gave him little books to read prayers from. She took a tiny blue medal out of her pocket and handed it to me. That night I pinned it to my vest and always wore it there after that. Mr Gentleman laughed when he came to see it, months later.

'You might care to see the kitchen?' she asked, and I followed her out to the kitchen. There were white presses built-in along the walls and the wood range was replaced with an anthracite cooker. In the kitchen garden outside there were six or seven young nuns walking singly, with heads lowered as if they were meditating. I was waiting to hear Bull's-Eye chase the hens off the flag, but of course there were no hens to chase. The visit upset me more than I had expected, and things that I thought I had forgotten kept floating to the surface of my mind. The skill with which Hickey set the mousetraps and put them under the stairs. The smell of apple jelly in the autumn and the fly-paper hanging from the ceiling with black flies all over it. Flitches of bacon hung up to smoke. The cookery book on the window-ledge stained with egg yolk. These small things crowded in on me so I felt very sad going down the drive.

On the way down I thought I ought to go into the gate-lodge and see my father. I lifted the latch but the door was locked. And I was just going out the gate, feeling very relieved, when I heard him call, 'Who's there?'

He opened the door and was lifting his braces up on to his shoulders. He was in his bare feet.

'Oh, I was lying down for an hour. I had a bad aul head-ache.'

'Go on back to bed,' I said. I was praying that he would. 'Not at all. Come on in.' He shut the door behind me. The kitchen was small and smoky and the little white lace half-curtain on the window was the colour of cigarette ash. There were three enamel mugs on the table with tea leaves in each of them.

'Have a cup o' tea,' he said.

'All right.' I filled the kettle from the bucket on the floor, and spilt some water of course. I'm always clumsy when people are watching me do something. He sat down and put on his socks. His toenails needed to be cut.

'Where were you?' he asked.

'Up home.' It would always be home.

'Whojusee?' I told him.

'Was she asking for me?'

'No.'

'Her and I are the best of friends.'

'They have the house lovely,' I said, hoping that it would make him feel guilty.

'The grandest house in the country,' he said. 'I don't miss it at all,' he said then. And I thought of my mother at the bottom of the lake, and how enraged she'd be if she could only hear him.

'Anyhow I was robbed of it,' he said, scratching his forehead.

'So that's the story,' I thought.

'How were you robbed?' I asked, impertinently.

'Well, I was, you know. They all said when I inherited it from my grand-uncle that I wouldn't have it long. And they did their best to get me out of it.'

So that was the story now. And to strangers and people going the road in summer-time, he'd scratch his forehead, point to the big house, and tell them that he was robbed of it. I thought of Mama, and I could see her shaking her head, woefully. Always when I was with him, I thought of Mama.

The kettle boiled and water bubbled from the spout. I looked round for the teapot.

'Where's the teapot?'

'Oh, a cup will do the finest. It makes lovely tea,' and he instructed me to empty the tea leaves out of the enamel mugs. He told me how much tea to put into each mug and then I poured the boiling water into them and put them on a hot coal to draw. I added milk and sugar to his, but couldn't stir it, for fear of disturbing all the tea leaves at the bottom. Mine looked like boiled turf.

'Isn't that a marvellous cup o' tea I made,' he said. 'I made,' I thought.

''Tis all right,' I answered. Why was I so halting? I couldn't bring myself to be friendly.

'Finest tea in the country. The Connor girls were down here gathering mushrooms last year and they came in out of a shower, so I gave them a cup of that tea. They said they never drank anything like it.' I smiled and tried to look agreeable.

'Where's Bull's-Eye?'

'He's gone. He got poisoned.' Soon there would be nothing good left from the old life.

'How did he get poisoned?'

'There was strychnine down for foxes and he took it.'

'You should have complained about that,' I said. I was angry.

'Complain! Is it me to complain? Sure I never bothered anyone in my life.' I searched desperately for something to say. Quickly.

'Any news of Hickey?' I asked. I hadn't heard from him for two Christmases. Maisie said that he was engaged to someone, but we never heard whether he got married or not.

'Is it that fella? I never trusted him. Too good a time he had, wiping my eye like everyone else.' I looked into the cluster of tea leaves in the bottom of my mug and tried to foresee my future. I was looking for romance, thinking that next week I would be in Dublin, free from it all. He coughed, nervously. He was going to say something important. I trembled.

'There's something I want to say to you now, my lady; and I don't want you to get up on your high horses either.'

He took his teeth off the dresser and put them in. Felt better, more important, perhaps?

'You're to behave yourself in Dublin. Live decent. Mind your faith, and write to your father. I don't like the way you've turned out at all. Not one bit.'

''Tis mutual, most mutual,' I thought, but did not say so. I was afraid of getting struck and all I wanted was to get quickly out of the smoky kitchen. Even my eyes were hurting, and the damn' smoke made me cough.

'I'll be careful,' I said. I looked round for the clock, it was ticking but I couldn't see it. It was on the mantelpiece, face downwards. I lifted it up and said I was very sorry but I had to go, as tea was at half past five.

'I'll convey you over the road,' he said and he put on his boots. It was all right once we got out in the air, there were lots of other people around and I was not so afraid.

Molly was waxing the hail when I got in. The house was quiet.

'Where's Martha?'

'In the chapel, I suppose,' said Molly.

'The chapel?' Martha always sneered at religion, and praying and craw-thumpers.

'Oh yes, she's off every day now. Mass and everything,' Molly said.

'Since when?'

'Since the children's First Communion. She went up to see the dresses and got a fit o' crying in the chapel. Then she began to go to devotions after that, and in no time she was going to Mass.'

'That's funny,' I said, remembering Martha's remark once, that religion was dope for fools.

'Age changes people,' said Molly, shaking her head, like an old woman.

'How does it?'

'Ah, it softens them. They'll stick out for things when they're young. But when they get on, they get soft.'

'Will you marry your boy, Molly?' I asked. She seemed a little strange. Not like herself. Wise instead of cheerful.

'I suppose so.'

'Do you love him?'

'I'll tell you that when I'm married ten years.'

'Molly! How have you so much sense?' Molly could teach me things about life. I was ashamed of myself when I saw how sensible she was. She had a hard life and she never pitied herself, never felt sorry for herself like me.

'I had to have it. My mother died when I was nine and I had to rear two younger ones.'

'Wasn't she killed?' I said. I had heard some terrible story about her being burnt.

'Yeh. Burnt to death,' she said.

'How?' I asked, though of course I shouldn't have.

'It was near six, the potatoes weren't boiled for dinner, and the men were nearly home. We heard the cart coming in at the bottom of the lane. "Oh God," says she, "blow up the fire," and she threw paraffin on it and the fire flared up into her face and she was a mass o' flames in two seconds. I threw a can o' milk on her but 'twas no use.' Molly told me this without crying, without breaking down; and I envied her for being so brave.

'We'll make a cup o' tea,' she said, getting up off her knees.

'If I drink any oftener this day, I'll overflow,' I said, but we went down to the kitchen and made a pot of tea and in a little while Martha came in. Afterwards, when Mr Brennan got home, Martha went upstairs with him to wash his hair. They were laughing and talking in the bathroom and when I was passing I saw her rubbing the short black hairs, briskly, between two halves of a towel. He was sitting on the bath and he had his arms round her bottom, with his head buried in her stomach. I was delighted to see them friendly.

'Maybe they'll be happy,' I thought and I hoped they would. Though in a way I was ashamed to see married people embrace each other. Because Mama and Dada never did.

When I went into the room I let a shout out of me. Baba was prostrate on the bed, with a mass of white mud all over her face.

'Oh!' I yelled, and Molly ran up to know what was wrong.

'Christ, you're a bloody aul eejit,' Baba said. 'I have my French mud-pack on, preparing for Dublin. Did you never hear of it?' she asked. Her voice was stiff, because of the stuff round her lips, she couldn't move them properly.

'No,' I said, sullenly. I hated being such a fool.

'You're a right-looking eejit,' she said, as she sat up and reached to the dressing-table for a wet sponge and bowl of water.

'Your mam and dad are great friends,' I whispered.

'Yeh. Before she knows where she is she'll have a damn' child or something.'

'Would you mind?' I asked.

'Like hell. Bloody sure I'd mind. I'd be the laughingstock of the whole country. What would Norman Spalding say?' Norman Spalding was the bank manager's son, and Baba was doing a line with him. Just for the few days, before we left for Dublin. She said that the boys round home were little squirts anyhow, and no use. Sometimes during the holidays I made dates with some of them but when I was out with them I was bored, and when they held my hand I felt disgusted. I always wanted to rush back to Mr Gentleman, he was so much nicer than young boys.

All that week we prepared for Dublin.

On the last day I went up the village to say good-bye to a few people and to buy a packet of labels.

There was a pig fair around the market-house. There were carts and red turf-creels outside the shops and pink baby pigs in nests of straw, squeaking in the back of the creels. The pigs grunted and stuck their noses through the holes in the creels, trying to get out.

It was another wild, windy day with dust blowing up the street and wisps of straw and torn paper. On the wind came the smell that prevails at every country fair. The pleasant smell of fresh dung, the warm smell of animals, and old clothes, and tobacco smoke.

The wind got inside the heavy top-coats of the farmers and flapped them out so that they looked like men in a storm; they looked fierce, as they argued about prices and spat on their palms and argued more.

Two men came out of Jack Holland's. The commotion and tobacco smoke came out with them, when they held the door open for a second, and more men smelt the noise and the porter and went in hurriedly. Mountainy children stood around minding donkeys, and waiting for their fathers. Their clothes were too big for them and they looked foolish. Their large eyes noticed everything, their gaze followed the women who came out of the houses and crossed over to fill a bucket of water from the green pump. The mountainy children looked at the untidy village women with surprise and the village women looked back with that certain disdain which villagers have for poor mountainy people.

Tommy Tuohey was weighing pigs on the big scales outside the little market-house and the pigs were screaming to get away. It was dark and there were black storm clouds racing across the sky. Everyone said it would rain.

I bought the labels and said good-bye to Jack. The shop was full and there was no time to call me aside and whisper things to me. Fortunately.

I was not sorry to be leaving the old village. It was dead and tired and old and crumbling and falling down. The shops needed paint and there seemed to be fewer geraniums in the upstairs windows than there had been when I was a child.

The next hour flew. Once again we were saying good-bye. Martha cried. I suppose she felt that *we* were always going; and that life stood still for her. Life had passed her by, cheated her. She was just forty.

We were in a third-class carriage that said 'No Smoking', and the train chugged along towards Dublin.

'Chrisake, where's there a smoking-carriage?' Baba asked. Her father had put us on the train, but we didn't let on that we each had a packet of cigarettes in our handbags.

'We'll look for one,' I said and we went down the corridor, giggling and giving strangers the 'So what' look. I suppose it was then we began that phase of our lives as the giddy country girls brazening the big city. People looked at us and then looked away again, as though they had just discovered that we were naked or something. But we didn't care. We were young and, we thought, pretty.

Baba was small and thin, with her hair cut short like a boy's; and little tempting curls falling on to her forehead. She was neat-looking and any man could lift her up in his arms and carry her off. But I was tall and gawky, with a bewildered look, and a mass of bewildered auburn hair.

'We'll have sherry or cider or some damn' thing,' she said, turning round to face me. Her skin was dark and when she smiled I thought of autumn things, like nuts and russet-coloured apples.

'You're lovely looking,' I said.

'You're gorgeous,' she said, in return.

'You're a picture,' I said.

'You're like Rita Hayworth,' she said. 'D'you know what I often think?'

'What?'

'How the poor bloody nuns managed the day you kept them out of the lavatory.'

At the mention of the convent, I got a faint smell of cabbage; that smell that lingered in every corner of the school.

''Twas tough on them, holding it,' she said, and she let out one of her mad, donkey laughs.

The train turned a sharp bend and we fell on to the nearest seat. Baba was laughing, so I smiled at a man opposite. He was half asleep, and didn't notice me. We got up and went down the aisle of the carriages, between the dusty velvet-covered seats. In a while we came to the bar.

'Two glasses of sherry,' Baba said, blowing smoke directly into the barman's face.

'What kind?' he asked. He was friendly and didn't mind the smoke.

'Any kind.' He filled two glasses and put them on the

counter. After we had drunk the sherry I bought cider for us, and we were a little tipsy as we swayed on the high stools and looked out at the rain as it fell on the fields that shot past the train. But being tipsy we did not see very much and the rain did not touch us.

14

We got in to Dublin just before six. It was still bright, and we carried our bags across the platform, stopping for a minute to let others pass by. We had never seen so many people in our lives.

Baba hailed a taxi and told the driver our new address. It was written on the label of her suitcase. We had got lodgings through an advertisement in the paper and our future landlady was a foreigner.

'Jesus, Cait, this is life,' Baba said, relaxing in the back seat, as she took out a hand-mirror to look at herself. She brought a lock of hair down on to her forehead and it looked well there, falling over one eyebrow.

I remember nothing of the streets we drove through. They were all too strange. At six the bells rang out from some church which were followed by other bells, with other chimes, ringing from churches all over the city. The peals of the bells mingled together and were in keeping with the fresh spring evening, and there was a special comfort in their toll. I liked them already.

We passed a cathedral, whose dark stone was still wet from the afternoon rain, though the streets were dry. We were dizzy trying to see the clothes in the shop windows.

'Christ, there's a gorgeous frock in that window. Hey, sir,' she yelled, leaning forward in the seat.

The driver, without looking back, pushed a sliding window that separated the front of the car from the back.

'D'ju say something?' He had the sing-song accent that is spoken in County Cork.

'Are you from Cork?' Baba said, sniggering. He pretended not to hear and closed the sliding window. Then, soon after, he turned to the left, drove down an avenue, and we were there. We got out and split the fare between us. We knew nothing about tipping. He left the cases on the footpath outside the gate. There was a motor-bike against the railings and inside a narrow concrete path ran between two small squares of cut grass. Between the grass and the path was an oblong flower bed, at either side, and a few sallow snowdrops wilted in the damp clay. The house itself was red-brick, two storey, with a bay window downstairs.

Baba gave a cheeky knock on the chromium knocker and rang the bell at the same time.

'Oh God, Baba, don't be impatient like that.'

'None o' your cowardy-custard nonsense,' she said, winking at me. The lock of hair was very rakish. There were milk bottles beside the foot-scraper and I heard someone come up the hallway.

The door was opened and we were greeted by a woman in thick-lensed glasses, who wore a brown knitted dress and knitted, hairy, grey stockings.

'Ah, you are the welcome,' she said, and called upstairs, 'Gustav, they're here.'

There were white mackintoshes on the hall stand and a coloured umbrella that reminded me of a postcard Miss Moriarty sent me from Rome. We took off our coats.

She was a low-sized woman, and was almost the width of the dining-room doorway. Her bottom was like the bottom of a woman in a funny postcard. It was a mountain in itself. We followed her into the dining-room.

It was a small room crowded with walnut furniture. There was a piano in one corner and next to it was a sideboard that had framed photographs on top of it, and opposite that was a china cabinet. It was stuffed with glasses, cups, mugs, and all sorts of souvenirs. Sitting at the table was a bald, middle-aged man eating a boiled egg. He held it in one hand and spooned the contents out with the other hand. He looked very funny holding the egg on his lap as if he weren't supposed to be eating it. He greeted us in some foreign accent and went on with his tea. He was not handsome. His eyes were too close together and he looked somehow treacherous.

We sat down. The circular table was covered with a green velvet cloth that was tasselled at the edges and there was a vase of multi-coloured everlasting anemones in the middle of the table.

Something about the room, perhaps the velvet cloth, or the cluttered china cabinet, or perhaps the period of the furniture, reminded me of my mother and of our house as it had once been.

Our landlady brought in two small plates of cooked ham, some buttered bread, and a small dish of jam.

'Gustav,' she called again, as she came in the dining-room. I was a little afraid of her. Her voice was brutal and commandeering.

'Very good, my own make, home-made,' she said, putting a fancy spoon into the jam.

We ate quickly and ravenously and when we had cleared

the bread plate we looked at one another and at the bald man opposite us. He had finished eating and was reading a foreign paper.

'Joanna,' he called and she came in, drying her hands in her flowered apron. He said something in a foreign language to her. I supposed it was to ask for more bread.

'Mine Got Almighty save us! Country girls have a big huge appetite,' she said, raising her hands in the air. They were fat hands and roughened from years of work. She had a marriage ring and an eternity ring. Poor Gustav.

She went out and the man continued reading.

Baba and I were certain that he didn't understand English. So while we were waiting for the bread, Baba did a little mime act. Bowing to me, she begged in a trembling voice, 'Oh, lady divine, will you pass me the wine?' I passed her the bottle of vinegar.

'Put on the tea-cosy,' she said; and christened me 'lady supreme'. Then in another voice, she pleaded, 'Oh, lady supreme, will you pass me the cream?' and I passed her the milk jug. Then she turned towards him, though he was hidden behind the paper and said, 'You bald-headed scutter, will you pass me the butter?' and while we were grinning, his hand came out from behind the newspaper and slowly he pushed the empty butter-dish in her direction. We laughed more and saw that his hands were shaking. He was laughing too. It was a nice beginning.

Joanna brought back two more slices of bread and some small pieces of cake. It was cake with two colours. Half yellow, half chocolate. Mama called it marble cake but Joanna had some other name for it. The pieces were cunningly cut. Each piece only a mouthful. The man opposite took two pieces and Baba kicked me under the table as if to warn me to eat quickly. She stuffed her own mouth full.

Gustav came in and we stood up to shake hands with him. He was a small, pale-faced man with cunning eyes and an apologetic smile. His hands were white and refined looking.

'No, ladies, stay be sitting,' he said humbly, too humbly. I preferred Joanna. Baba was delighted that he called us ladies, and she gave him one of her loganberry smiles.

'Up there shaving all the night. What you got your new shirt on for?' Joanna said, looking carefully at his shirt and the top of his waistcoat. He said that he was going down to the local.

'Just for a small time, Joanna,' he said.

'Mine Got! I have two chickens to pluck and you not help me.' The smile never left his face.

'Nice, nice ladies,' he said, pointing to us, and Baba was fluttering her eyelashes at a furious rate.

'Oh yes, yes; eat; eat up,' Joanna said suddenly, remembering us. But there was nothing else to eat as we had cleared the table.

I began to tidy up the things, and pile the plates on top of one another but Baba said in my ear: 'Christ's sake, we'll be doing it day and night if we begin once. Skivvies, that's what we'll be.' So I took her advice and followed her upstairs to the bedroom where Gustav had put our cases.

It was a small room that looked out on the street. There was dark brown linoleum on the floor and a beaded lampshade over the electric bulb that hung from the ceiling.

The window opened out on the street and I went over to smell the city air and see what it looked like. There were children down below, playing hopscotch, and picky beds. One boy had a mouth-organ and he put it to his lips and played whenever he felt like it. Seeing me they all stared up, and one, the biggest one, asked: 'What time is it?' I was smoking a cigarette and pretended not to hear him. 'Eh, miss, what time is it? Thirty-two degrees is freezing point, what's squeezing point?'

You could hear Baba laughing at the dressing-table and she told me for Christ's sake to come in or we'd be thrown out. She said he was great gas, and we must get to know him.

The wardrobe was empty but we couldn't hang our clothes because we had forgotten to bring hangers. So we laid them across the big armchair in the corner of the room.

At the gate below a motor-bicycle started up and went roaring down the avenue. Gustav was gone.

In the next room a man began to play a fiddle.

'Jesus,' Baba said, simply, and put her hands to her ears. She was walking round the room with her hands to her ears, swearing, when Joanna knocked and came in.

'Herman, he does to practise,' she said, smiling, when Baba pointed with her thumb towards the other room.

'Very talent. A musician. You like music?' and Baba said we adored music, and that we had come all the way to Dublin to hear a man playing a fiddle.

'Oh, nice. Good. Very nice,' and Baba made a gesture which told me that she thought Joanna was nuts. I was still unpacking so Joanna came over and looked at my clothes. She asked me if my father was rich and Baba chimed in and said he was a millionaire.

'A millionaire?' You could see her pupils get large, behind her thick lenses.

'My charge too cheap then, hah?' she said, grinning at us. Her way of grinning was unfortunate. It was thick and stupid and made you hate her. But perhaps it was the glasses.

'No. Too dear,' Baba said.

'Dear? Darling? Kliena? I not understand.'

'No. Too costly,' I said, catching my hair up with a ribbon and hoping before I consulted the mirror that it would make my face beautiful.

'You happy?' she asked, suddenly anxious, suddenly worried in case we should leave.

'We happy,' I said, for both of us, and she grinned. I liked her.

'I give you a present,' she said. We looked at one another in astonishment as she went out of the room.

She came back with a bottle of something yellow and two thimble-sized glasses. They were glasses such as the chemist had at home. They were for measuring medicines. She poured some of the thick yellow liquid into each glass.

'Your health here. Hah!' she said. We put the glasses to our lips.

'Good?' she asked, before we had tasted it at all.

'Good,' I said, lying. It was eggy and had a sharp spirit taste besides.

'Mine.' She put her hand across her stout chest. Her breasts were not defined; she was one solid front of outstanding chest.

'On the Continent we make our own. Parties, everything, we make our own.'

'God protect us from the Continent,' Baba said to me in Irish, and was smiling so that her two dimples showed.

I had put a jar of face cream and a small bottle of Evening in Paris perfume on the table, to make the room habitable, and Joanna went over to admire them. She took the lid off the cream jar and smelt it. Then she smelt the perfume.

'Nice,' she said, still smelling the contents of the dusky-blue perfume bottle.

'Have some,' I said, because we were under a compliment to her for the little drink.

'Expensive? Is it expensive?'

'Costs pounds,' Baba said, smirking into her glass. Baba was going to make a fool of Joanna, I could see that.

'Pounds. Mine Got!' She screwed the metal cork back on the bottle and laid it down quickly. In case it should break.

'Tomorrow perhaps I have some. Tomorrow Sunday. You Catholics?'

'Yes. Are you?' Baba asked.

'Yes, but we on the Continent are not so rigid as you Irish.' She shrugged her shoulders to show a certain indifference. Her knitted dress was uneven at the tail and sagged at both sides. She went out and we heard her go downstairs.

'What will we do, Gait?' Baba asked as she lay full length on the single bed.

'I don't know. Will we go to Confession?' It was what we usually did on Saturday evenings.

'Confession. Christ, don't be such a drip, we'll go down town. Oh God, isn't it Heaven?' She kicked her feet up in the air and hugged the pillow that was under the chenille bedspread.

'Put on everything you've got,' she said. 'We'll go to a dance.'

'So soon?'

'Christ, so soon! Soon, and we cooped up in that gaol for three thousand years.'

'We don't know the way.' I wasn't really interested in dancing. At home I walked on the boys' toes and couldn't

165

turn corners so well. Baba danced like a dream, spinning round and round until her cheeks were flushed and her hair blown every way.

'Go down and use your elegant English on Frau Buxomburger.'

'That's not nice,' I said, putting on my wistful face. The face Mr Gentleman liked best.'

'Christ, she's gas, isn't she? I keep expecting that her old arse will drop off. Looks like one that's stuck on.'

'Ssh, ssh,' I said. I was afraid the fiddler would hear us as he had stopped sawing.

'Go down and ask, and stop this ssh-ing business.'

Joanna was pouring a kettle of scalding water over a dead Rhode Island Red chicken. When the bird was completely wet she began to tear the feathers away. I was in the kitchen watching her, but she hadn't heard me because there was ceilidh music being played on the wireless.

The dead chicken reminded me of all our Sunday dinners at home. Hickey would wring a chicken's neck on Saturday morning, leave it outside the back door and it would stir and make an effort to move itself for a long time after it was killed. Bull's-Eye, thinking it was alive, would bark at it and try to chase it away.

'Mine Got! you give me a fright,' she said, turning round, as she held the chicken in one hand. I said I was very sorry and asked her the way down town. She told me but her instructions were very confusing and I knew that we would have to ask somebody else on the street.

When I came upstairs Baba had gone out to the bathroom, and without her the room was cheerless and empty. Outside in the avenue it was evening. The children were gone. The street was lonesome. A child's handkerchief blew on one of the spears of our railing. There were houses stretching across the plain of city, houses separated by church spires, or blocks of flats, ten and twenty storeys high. In the distance the mountains were a brown blur with clouds resting on them. They were not mountains really but hills. Gentle, memorable hills.

As I looked towards them, I thought of lambs being born in the cold and in the dark, of sheep farmers trudging down across the hills, and afterwards I thought of the shepherds and their dogs stretching out in front of the fire, to doze for an hour until it was time to go out again and face the sharp wind. Our farm was not on the mountain, but four or five miles away there were mountains, where Hickey brought me once on the cross-bar of his bicycle. He put a cushion on the bar, in case my bottom got sore. We went for a sheep-dog. It was early spring with lambs being born, and you could hear them bleating pitifully against the wind. We got the sheep-dog. A handful of black and white fur, asleep in a box of hay. He grew up to be Bull's-Eye.

'Will you come a-waltzing, Matilda, with me; waltzing, Matilda,' Baba sang behind my back, and drew me into a waltz.

'What in the hell are you thinking about?' she asked. But she did not wait to hear.

'I've a smashing idea. I'll change my name. I'll be Barbara, pronounced "Baubra". Sounds terrific, doesn't it? Pity you're going to work in that damn' shop. 'Twill cramp our style,' she said thoughtfully.

'Why?'

'Oh, every little country mohawk is in a bloody grocer's. We'll say you're at college if anyone asks.'

'But who's to ask?'

'Fellows; we'll have them swarming round us. And, mind you, Christ, if you take any fellow of mine I'll give you something to cry about.'

'I won't,' I said, smiling, admiring the big wide sleeves of my blouse and wondering if he would notice it and wondering too when himself and Mrs Gentleman would return home.

'Your cigarette, your cigarette,' I said to Baba. She had left it on the bedside table and it had burnt a mark in from the edge. You could smell the burnt wood.

'Mine Got! What you mean?' Joanna said, bursting in without knocking.

'My best table, my table,' she said, rushing over to examine the burn-mark. I was crimson with fear.

'Smoking, young girls, it is forbid,' she said; there were tears in her eyes as she threw the cigarette into the fireplace.

'We must have an ashtray,' Baba said, and then she looked at the little bamboo table and got down on her knees to look under it.

'It's useless anyhow, it's reeking with worms,' she said to Joanna.

'What you mean?' Joanna was breathing terribly hard as if she were going to erupt.

'Woodworm,' Baba said and Joanna jumped and said it was impossible. But in the end Baba won and Joanna took the table away and brought it out to a shed in the yard.

'Please, ladies, not to lie on the good bedspreads, they are from the Continent, pure chenille,' she said, imploringly, and I promised that we would be more careful.

'Now we have no table,' I said to Baba, when Joanna went out.

'So what?' she asked, as she took off her dress.

'Was it wormy?' I asked.

'How the hell would I know?' she began to spray deodorant under her arms. Her neck was not as white as mine. I was pleased.

We got ready quickly and went down into the neon fairyland of Dublin. I loved it more than I had ever loved a summer's day in a hayfield. Lights, faces, traffic, the enormous vitality of people hurrying to somewhere. A dark-faced woman, in an orange silk thing, went by.

'Christ, they're in their underwear here,' Baba said. The woman had enormous dark eyes, with dark shadows under them. She seemed to be searching the night and the crowd for something poignant. Something to equal the beauty of the shadows and her carved, cat-like face.

'Isn't she beautiful?' I said to Baba.

'She's like something dug up,' Baba said as she crossed over to look in the glass door of an ice-cream parlour.

A doorman opened it, and held it open. So there was nothing for us to do but to go in.

We had two large dishes of ice-cream. It was served with peaches and cream; and the whole lot was decorated with flaked chocolate. There were songs, pouring out of a metal box, near our table. Baba tapped her feet and swayed her shoulders, keeping time with the melody. Afterwards she put money in the slot herself and played the same songs over again.

'Jesus, we're living at last,' she said. She was looking round to see if there were any nice boys at the other tables.

'It's nice,' I said. I meant it. I knew now that this was the place I wanted to be. For evermore I would be restless for crowds and lights and noise. I had gone from the sad noises, the lonely rain pelting on the galvanized roof of the chicken-house; the moans of a cow in the night, when her calf was being born under a tree.

'Are we going dancing?' Baba asked. My feet were tired and I told her so. We went home and bought a bag of chips in a shop quite near our avenue. We ate them going along the pavement. The lights overhead were a ghastly green.

'Jesus, you look like someone with consumption,' Baba said, as she handed me a chip.

'So do you,' I said. And together we thought of a poem that we had learnt long ago. We recited it out loud:

'From a Munster Vale they brought her
From the pure and balmy air,
An Ormond Ullin's daughter
With blue eyes and golden hair.
They brought her to the city
And she faded slowly there,
For consumption has no pity
For blue eyes and golden hair.'

There were people looking at us, but we were too young to care. Baba blew into the empty chip-bag until it was puffed out. Then she bashed it with her fist, and it burst making a tremendous noise.

'I'm going to blow up this town,' she said and she meant it, that first night in Dublin.

170

15

It was a clear spring day when I drew back the dusty cretonne curtains to let the sun into our bedroom on Monday morning. The room seemed shabby, now that I knew it better. The linoleum was worn thin and Joanna had brought up an orange box and stood it on end between our two beds. She had covered it with a strip of cretonne that matched the curtains but no matter how it was covered it was still only an orange box.

'Breakfast,' she called as she knocked loudly on the bedroom door. Baba was asleep. She said she was going to miss college the first day because we had been dancing the night before and went to bed late. The room was untidy, there were clothes strewn all over the floor and already the dressing-table had a film of powder on it. It was nice to see the room so untidy. We were grown up and independent.

I came downstairs and found Herman, the bald-headed lodger, eating some raw minced steak.

'Good for a man,' he said, smiling and tapping his chest to show how healthy he was. He did physical exercises morning and night and Baba and I listened outside his door while he counted and thrust his arms and legs into the atmosphere.

'No egg, thank you,' I said to Joanna when she brought it

in to me. Baba said that all the eggs in the city were rotten, and more than likely we'd find a dead chicken inside soon as we topped one. I took her advice and got a disgust against all eggs, even against the little brown pullets' eggs that Hickey coddled for me, long ago.

I ate quickly and set out, just before nine. Gustav wished me luck and saw me to the door.

'Gustav, come watch your toast,' Joanna called, so he waved and shut the door very quietly.

The grocery shop was only a five-minute walk. There were trees along the footpath, and it was a soft day. The buds had thrust their way to the very tips of the thin, black, melancholy birch branches. The buds were lime-green and the branches black, slender branches stirring in the wind. There were pigeons on the chimney tops, and pigeons walking assuredly over the grey, sloping roofs. They were cheeky pigeons, who didn't mind the traffic. It was funny to watch them do their droppings, it squirted out easily and happily. I had never been so close to pigeons before.

My shop was in a shopping centre, between a drapery and a chemist's.

Tom Burns – Grocery was written over the door and painted crookedly on the window was a sign which read *Home-cooked ham a speciality*. There were fancy biscuit tins in the window and posters of girls eating crunchies. Nice girls with healthy teeth.

I went in, nervously. Behind the counter stood a stout man with a brown moustache. He was weighing bags of sugar, and he scooped the sugar out of a big sack.

'I'm the new girl,' I said.

'Oh, you're welcome,' he said, as he shook hands with me. I followed him in to the back of the shop. It was very untidy, with cardboard boxes littered all over the floor. Sitting on a high stool, copying bills from a large ledger, was a woman whom he introduced as his wife. She was wearing a white shop-coat.

'Ah, darling, you're welcome,' she said, as she swivelled round on the stool and faced me.

'Isn't she lovely?' she said to him. 'Oh, darling you're as welcome as the flowers in May. Gorgeous hair and everything.' She stroked my hair and I thanked her. Outside in the shop someone tapped the glass counter impatiently with a coin and Mr Burns went out.

'Any empty boxes?' I heard a child's voice ask; and he must have shaken his head because light footsteps went out the door.

Mrs Burns was smiling at me. She had a pale, round face and sleepy, tobacco eyes. She was fat (though not as comically fat as Joanna) and lazy-looking.

'Darling, did you bring your shop-coat?' I said that I hadn't heard about one and she said: 'Oh, darling, how terrible, he should have told you. He's so forgetful, he forgets to charge people for things.'

I said that was a pity and tried to look sympathetic.

'Darling, there's a drapery two doors away. Maybe you'd like to nip out and get one. Tell Mrs Doyle I sent you.'

'I have no money,' I said. I had spent ten shillings at the dance the previous night. (It cost me five shillings to go in, another shilling to put my coat in the cloakroom, and I drank three minerals because nobody asked me to dance after I fell. I fell dancing a barn dance. I must have tripped over my partner's shoes; anyhow I fell and my flared skirt blew up around me, so that people saw my garters and things. Baba looked away as if she didn't know me and my partner slunk off towards the bandstand. It was an awful moment. Then I got up, smoothed my skirt and went upstairs. I sat on the balcony, and drank minerals for the rest of the night. I tried to look casual as hell, to show that I wasn't interested in dancing anyhow. Down below Baba was drifting under the soft pink lights and hundreds of boys and girls were dancing cheek to cheek up and down the ballroom under the twists of coloured papers that hung from the ceiling and moved to a music of their own. Waltzing was forgetfulness and I wished that Mr Gentleman would suddenly appear out of nowhere and steer me through the strange, long, sweet night, and say things in my ear and keep his arms round me, even when the music stopped and the girls went back to their seats until the music struck up and they were asked for the next dance.)

'Well, darling, you better wait so, until you get paid on Saturday,' Mrs Burns said churlishly. She folded her thin lips inwards so that you thought she had none. She was displeased.

Mr Burns told me to weigh bags of tea and sugar: and after that he said I could weigh half-pounds of streaky rashers.

'Tom, I think I'll make the bed now and get a few hams on,' his wife said and disappeared for the rest of the morning. He filled the shelves with tins of peas and bottles of relish and all the time he talked to me. He told me he was a countryman and how much he loved the country, and the Sundays long ago in Galway when he played hurley. Very long ago, I thought to myself.

'I go back there every year. Last year I helped them cut the turf,' he said. And in that instant I saw Hickey's boot on a slane, cutting a sod from the black-brown turf bank. When he dug the slane into the bank, water squelched out and flowed down into the pool of black bog water. I saw the bog water and the bog lilies and the blackened patches of ground where we had made fires to boil a kettle, and the heather which brushed my ankles and the great limestone ridges that rose out of the brown and purple earth. Often, while Flickey was cutting or footing the turf, I used to wander away over to the bog-lake, picking my steps from one limestone rock to the next. The edge of the bog-lake was fringed with bulrushes and at certain times of the year their heads were a soft, brown plush. And at other times of the year, flowers came on the waterlily leaves. Wax flowers, swaying, on the flat green saucer leaves. Pretty flowers that no one ever saw because the men cutting turf were too busy. The rushes were lonesome; when the wind cried through them the cry was like the curlew, and the curlew was the Uileann pipe that Billy Tuohey played in the evenings. At the far edge of the lake there was a belt of poplar trees, shutting out the world. The world I wanted to escape into. And now that I had come into the world, that scene of bogs and those country faces were uppermost in my thoughts.

'Oh God, I'm sorry,' I said. In my daydreaming I had let the sack of sugar fall sideways and the sugar was flowing on to the floor. The wood floor was dusty, so I couldn't recover the sugar. He sent me into the kitchen for the brush and the dustpan.

Mrs Burns was drinking tea and she had an open tin of fancy biscuits on the table. The hams were simmering in big black pots on top of the coal range. She had put apples and cloves in the water and the smell was delicious.

'I came in for the dustpan,' I said.

'It's over there beside the range. Are you doing a little cleaning, darling?' Her eyes brightened.

'No. I spilt sugar.' I wouldn't have told her but I was afraid that Mr Burns might mention it when she asked him in bed that night what he thought of me.

'Oh, darling angel, how much sugar?' Her face changed its expression and once again her lips disappeared.

'Just a little,' I said placatingly.

'Now you must learn to be careful. Mr Burns and I never waste a thing. Now, darling, you will be careful?' Never waste a thing and she stuffing herself with biscuits.

'I will,' I said. I wasn't looking at her suet-pale face but at the top button of her yellow jersey dress. It was an expensive dress but stained all over. She had a pencil over her ear and the point of it showed through her grey-black hair. She was about fifty.

Later on in the morning the daily help came. Mr Burns introduced me to her. Her name was Joe. A withered little woman in a black coat and a black hat that was going green. She disappeared into the hallway and I heard her coughing. She had a bad cough. A cigarette cough she told me afterwards.

The messenger boy came at eleven.

'Willie, you're late again,' Mr Burns said, looking up at the railway clock that was fixed to the wall.

'My mother is sick, sir,' Willie said, saying mudder for mother.

He had a comb and a mouth-organ in his breast pocket and he got the sweeping-brush and began to brush the floor languidly. That was the entire household, except for the sleek black cat that I dreaded. Mr Burns told me that he locked her into the shop at night as there were a lot of mice

176

around. At half past eleven he went inside for a cup of tea.

'Hello,' Willie said, winking lightly at me. We were friends.

'Is she up?' he asked.

'Who?'

'Mrs Burns.'

'Oh yes, hours ago.'

'She's a right old hag. She wouldn't give you a fright.'

('Froight' was the way Willie pronounced it.)

'Do we get tea?' I whispered. I was thinking of the biscuits and the one I would choose first; and if she was likely to pass me the tin twice.

'Tea, my eye.' (Moy oy.) A customer came in for a large packet of corn-flakes and Willie got them down for me. They were high up on a shelf and he had to mount the step ladder. It was a shaky-looking ladder and I got dizzy just watching him climb.

Then he showed me where things were kept, cloves and Vick and currants and packet soups and all the little things that I might miss. On a postcard I wrote down the prices of obvious things like tea and sugar and butter and the morning dragged on slowly until the angelus rang. Willie laughed while he was praying. Then he took a pin-up girl out of his pocket and said, 'She's like you, Miss Brady.' I was four or five years older than Willie so I didn't mind what he said.

'Peckish, darling?' Mrs Burns asked as she came out. I said yes, but in fact Willie and I had eaten two doughnuts and sugar barley while Mr Burns was having his tea. I put the money for them in the till. It was an elaborate metal till, and every time you opened the drawer it gave a sharp ring, so that you couldn't open the drawer secretly. Across the front of it were little buttons with numbers on them, and you had to press the numbers, depending on how much money you put in.

My fingers were sticky from weighing sugar, so I asked if I may go upstairs to wash my hands. I was dying to see upstairs. Their bedroom door was half open. I could see part of the carpeted floor, and the unmade bed with the pile of fluffy, soft, pink blankets on it. There was a box of chocolates beside the bed, on a wicker table, and copies of a magazine called *Field and Stream*.

The bathroom was untidy, with towels thrown on the floor and two open tins of talcum powder on the washbasin ledge. I washed myself and had a free sprinkle of lavender talc.

Downstairs in the hall, while I was putting on my coat, I could see Mrs Burns examining two plates of dinner which Joe, the cleaning woman, had got ready. There was chicken and potato salad on both plates. Mrs Burns took the breast of chicken off one plate and put it on the other plate. Then she put a leg on the plate which she had raided. She sat down to table and began to eat from the plate that had the white delicate meat. I coughed to let her know that I was there.

'Tell Mr Burns to lock up and come in for lunch. The creature, he must be starved,' she said. 'The creature,' I thought, and wondered if he ever caught her fiddling with the dinner plates.

'All right, Mrs Burns. 'Bye, 'bye now.'

'Good-bye, darling.' Her mouth was full.

I went over to my new home, wondering about the Burnses and their life together. I bet that she ate chocolates in bed and had three hot-water bottles, and while she was eating, Mr Burns was turned on his side reading *Field and Stream;* and the sleek cat downstairs was devouring frightened mice in the dark.

16

Easter was a month later. There were lilies in the window of the flower shop at the corner and there were purple sheets covering the statues in the chapel. On Good Friday the shops were closed and every place was sad. Purple-sad. Death-sad. Baba said we might as well be dead, so we cleaned our bedroom and went to bed early. I liked reading but Baba couldn't bear to see me reading. She'd pace about the room and ask me questions and read a passage over my shoulders and finally say it was 'bloody rubbish'.

Easter Saturday night, after I got paid, I went to Confession and then came down to Miss Doyle's drapery and bought a pair of nylons, a brassière, and a white lace handkerchief. The handkerchief was one I'd never use, never dare to; it was spider's web in the sunlight; frail and exquisite. I looked forward to the summer when I would wear it stuck into Mama's silver bracelet, with the lace frill hanging down, temptingly, over the wrist. Out boating with Mr Gentleman it would blow away, moving like a white lace bird across the surface of the blue water, and Mr Gentleman would pat my arm and say, 'We'll get another.' There was still no news of him, though Martha said in a letter that he had come home and was as brown as a berry from all the sun.

The brassière I bought was cheap. Baba said that once brassières were washed they lost their elasticity, so we might as well buy cheap ones and wear them until they got dirty. We threw the dirty ones in the dustbin but later we found that Joanna brought them back in and washed them.

'Christ, she'll re-sell them to us,' Baba said, and bet me sixpence; but Joanna didn't. She put them in the linen press and said that they would be useful. We thought she'd put pieces in at the side, and make them bigger, so that they fitted her. But she didn't. Next time, when the woman came to scrub, Joanna gave her the brassières instead of money. She was thrift itself. Mending. Patching. She ripped an old faded cardigan that had shrunk, and used the wool to knit bedsocks for Gustav. Her knitting was under the cushion of the armchair, and one day when Herman was drunk he disturbed the knitting. The stitches fell off the needle, crawled off the needle like little brown beetles, and settled on the cushion.

'Mine Got!' Joanna flew into a temper, her blood pressure soared, and her head began to spin. We carried her (oh the weight and the indecency of it) on to the sofa in the drawing-room. The drawing-room was never used. There were preserved eggs in a bucket on the floor and along the window seat there were apples. Some of them were bad, and the room had a pleasant cider smell. Herman gave her a spoonful of brandy, and she recovered and flew into a fresh rage.

'This room is sumptuous,' Baba said to Joanna. Baba went across to speak to the porcelain nymph in the fire-place. Joanna had rouged the nymph's cheeks and put nail polish on her finger-nails. She was a lollipop nymph.

'Will you fit on the brassière, Miss Brady?' the shop girl asked. Pale, First Communion voice; pale, pure, rosary-bead hands held the flimsy black sinful garment between her fingers and her fingers were ashamed.

'No. Just measure me,' I said. She took a measuring tape out of her overall pocket, and I raised my arms while she measured me.

The black underwear was Baba's idea. She said that we wouldn't have to wash it so often; and that it was useful if we ever had a street accident, or if men were trying to strip us in the backs of cars. Baba thought of all these things. I got black nylons too. I read somewhere that they were 'literary' and I had written one or two poems since I came to Dublin. I read them to Baba and she said they were nothing to the ones in mortuary cards.

'Good night, Miss Brady, happy Easter,' the First Communion voice said to me and I wished her the same.

When I came in they were all having tea. Even Joanna was sitting at the dining-room table, with tan make-up on her arms and a charm bracelet jingling on her wrist. Every time she lifted the cup the charms tinkled against the china, like ice in a cocktail glass. Cool, ice-cool, sugared cocktails. I liked them. Baba knew a rich man who bought us cocktails one evening.

There were stuffed tomatoes, sausage rolls, and simnel cake for tea.

'Good?' Joanna asked before I had swallowed the first mouthful of crumby pastry. I nodded. She was a genius at cooking, surprising us with things we had never seen, little yellow dumplings in soup, apple strudel, and sour cabbage, but how I wished that she didn't stand over us with imploring looks, asking 'Good?'.

'Tell jokes, my tell jokes?' Herman asked Gustav. He had taken a glass of wine, and always after a glass of wine he wanted to tell jokes.

Gustav shook his head. Gustav was pale and delicate. He looked unemployed, which of course was proper, because he did not go to work. He suffered from his nerves or something. I was never sure whether I liked Gustav or not. I don't think I liked the cunning behind his small blue eyes, and I often thought that he was too good to be true.

'Let him, tell jokes,' Joanna said; she liked to be made to laugh.

'No, we go to pictures. We have good time at pictures,' Gustav said, and Baba roared laughing and lifted her chair so that it was resting on its two back legs.

'There no juice at pictures,' Joanna said, and Baba's chair almost fell backwards, because she had got a fit of coughing on top of the laughing. She coughed a lot lately and I told her she ought to see about it.

'No juice' was Joanna's way of saying that the pictures were a waste of money.

'We go, Joanna,' Gustav said gently nudging her bare, tanned arm with his elbow. His shirt-sleeves were rolled up and his jacket was hanging on the back of his chair. It was a warm evening and the sun shone through the window and played with the apricot jam on the table.

'Yes, Gustav,' Joanna said. She smiled at him as she must have smiled when they were sweethearts in Vienna. She began to clear off the table and warned us about the good, best, china.

'Ladies come night-club with me?' Herman asked, jokingly.

'Ladies have date,' Baba said. She lowered her chin on to

her chest, to let me know that it was true. Her hair was newly set, so that it curved in soft black waves that lay like feathers on the crown of her head. I was raging. Mine was long and loose and silly-looking.

'More cake?' Joanna asked. But she had put the simnel cake into a marshmallow tin.

'Yes, please.' I was still hungry.

'Mine Got, you got too fat.' She made a movement with her hand, to outline big fat woman. She came back with a slice of sad sponge cake, that was probably put aside for trifle. I ate it.

Upstairs, I took off all my clothes and had a full view of myself in the wardrobe mirror. I was getting fat all right. I turned sideways, and looked round so that I could see the reflection of my hip. It was nicely curved and white like the geranium petals in the dressmaker's window-ledge.

'What's Rubenesque?' I asked Baba. She turned round to face me. She bad been painting her nails at the dressing-table.

'Chrisake, draw the damn' curtains or they'll think you're a sex maniac.' I ducked down on the floor, and Baba went over and drew the curtains. She caught the edges, nervously, between her thumb and her first finger, so that her nail polish would not get smudged. Her nails were salmon pink, like the sky which she had just shut out by drawing the curtain.

I was holding my breasts in my hands, trying to gauge their weight, when I asked her again, 'Baba what's Rubenesque?'

'I don't know. Sexy, I suppose. Why?' 'A customer said I was that.'

'Oh, you better be *it* all right, for this date,' she said.

'With whom?'

'Two rich men. Mine owns a sweet factory and yours has a stocking factory. Free nylons. Yippee. How much do your thighs measure?' She made piano movements with her fingers, so that the nail polish would dry quickly.

'Are they nice?' I asked tentatively. We had already had two disastrous nights, with friends that she had found. In the evenings, after her class, some other girls and herself went into a hotel, and drank coffee in the main lounge. Dublin being a small, friendly city, one or other of them was always bound to meet someone, and in that way Baba made a lot of acquaintances.

'Gorgeous. They're aged about eighty, and my fellow has every bit of himself initialled. Tie-pin, cuff-links, hand-kerchiefs, car cushions. The lot. He has leopards in his car as mascots.'

'I can't go, so,' I said, nervously.

'In Christ's name, why not?'

'I'm afraid of cats.'

'Look, Caithleen, will you give up the nonsense? We're eighteen and we're bored to death.' She lit a cigarette and puffed vigorously. She went on: 'We want to live. Drink gin. Squeeze into the front of big cars and drive up outside big hotels. We want to go places. Not to sit in this damp dump.' She pointed to the damp patch in the wallpaper, over the chimney-piece, and I was just going to interrupt her, but she got in before me. 'We're here at night, killing moths for Joanna, jumping up like maniacs every time a moth flies out from behind the wardrobe; puffing D.D.T. into crevices; listening to that lunatic next door playing the fiddle.' She sawed off her left wrist with her right hand. She sat on the bed exhausted. It was the longest speech Baba had ever made.

'Hear, hear,' I said, and I clapped. She blew smoke straight into my face.

'But we want young men. Romance. Love and things,' I said, despondently. I thought of standing under a street light in the rain with my hair falling crazily about, my lips poised for the miracle of a kiss. A kiss. Nothing more. My imagination did not go beyond that. It was afraid to. Mama had protested too agonizingly all through the windy years. But kisses were beautiful. His kisses. On the mouth, and on the eyelids, and on the neck when he lifted up the mane of hair.

'Young men have no bloody money. At least the gawks we meet. Smell o' hair-oil. Up the Dublin mountains for air, a cup of damp tea in a damp hostel. Then out in the woods after tea and a damp hand fumbling under your skirt. No, sir. We've had all the bloody air we'll ever need. We want life.' She threw her arms out in the air. It was a wild and reckless gesture. She began to get ready.

We washed and sprinkled talcum powder all over ourselves.

'Have some of mine,' Baba said, but I insisted, 'No, Baba, you have some of mine.' When we were happy we shared things, but when life was quiet and we weren't going anywhere, we hid our things like misers, and she'd say to me, 'Don't you dare touch my powder,' and I'd say, 'There must be a ghost in this room, my perfume was interfered with,' and she'd pretend not to hear me. We never loaned each other clothes then, and one worried if the other got anything new.

One morning Baba rang me at work and said, 'Jesus, I'll brain you when I see you.'

'Why?' The phone was in the shop and Mrs Burns was standing beside me, looking agitated.

'Have you my brassière on?'

'No I haven't,' I said.

'You must have; it didn't walk. I searched the whole damn' room and it isn't there.'

'Where are you now?'

'I'm in a phone-booth outside the college and I can't come out.'

'Why not?'

'Because I'm flopping all over the damn' place,' and I laughed straight into Mrs Burns's face and put down the phone.

'Oh, darling, I know how popular you must be. But tell your friends not to phone in the mornings. There might be orders coming through,' Mrs Burns said.

That night Baba found the brassière mixed up in the bedclothes. She never made her bed until evening.

We got ready quickly. I put on the black nylons very carefully so that none of the threads would get caught in my ring and then looked back to see if the seams were straight. They were bewitching. The stockings, not the seams. Baba hummed 'Galway Bay' and tied a new gold chain round the waist of her blue tweed dress.

I was still wearing my green pinafore dress and the white dancing-blouse. They smelt of stale perfume, all the perfume I had poured on before going to dances. I wished I had something new.

'I'm sick o' this,' I said, pointing to my dress. 'I think I won't go.'

So she got worried and loaned me a long necklace. I wound it round and round, until it almost choked me. The colour was nice next to my skin. It was turquoise and the beads were made of glass.

'My eyes are green tonight,' I said, looking into the mirror. They were a curious green, bright, luminous green, like wet lichen.

'Now mind – Baubra; and none of your Baba slop,' she warned me. She ignored the bit about my eyes. She was jealous. Mine were bigger than hers and the whites were a delicate blue, like the whites of a baby's eyes.

There was nobody in the house when we were going, out, so we put out the hall light and made sure that the door was locked. A gas-meter two doors down had been raided and Joanna warned us about locking up.

We linked and kept step with one another. There was a bus stop at the top of the avenue, but we walked on to the next stop. It was a penny cheaper from the next stop, to Nelson's Pillar. We had plenty of money that night, but we walked out of habit.

'What'll I drink?' I asked, and distantly somewhere in my head I heard my mother's voice accusing me, and I saw her shake her finger at me. There were tears in her eyes. Tears of reproach.

'Gin,' Baba said. She talked very loud. I could never get her to whisper and people were always looking at us in the streets, as if we were wantons.

'My ear-rings hurt,' I said.

'Take them off and give your ears a rest,' she said. Still aloud.

'But will there be a mirror?' I asked. I wanted to have them on when I got there. They were long giddy ear-rings and I loved shaking my head so that they dangled and their little blue glass stones caught the light.

'Yeh, we'll go into the cloaks first,' Baba said. I took them off and the pain in the lobes of my ears was worse. It was agony for a few minutes.

We passed the shop where I worked and the blind was drawn but there was a light inside. The blind wasn't exactly the width of the window; there was an inch to spare at either side and you could see the light through that narrow space.

'Guess what they're doing in there,' Baba said. She knew all about them and was always plying me with questions – what they ate and what kind of nightdresses were on the clothes-line and what he said to her when she said, 'Darling, I'll go up and make the bed now.'

'They're eating chocolates and counting the day's money,' I said. I could taste the liqueur chocolates Mr Gentleman gave me long ago.

'No they're not. They're taking a rasher off every half-pound you've weighed before going up to Confession,' she said, going over and trying to see through the slit at the corner. I saw a bus coming and we ran to the stop thirty or forty yards away.

'You're all dolled up,' the conductor said. He didn't' take our fares that night. We knew him from going in and out to town every other evening. We wished him a happy Easter.

17

The foyer of the hotel was brightly lit and there were palm plants in a huge vase over in one corner.

We went into the cloakroom first and I put on my earrings. We washed our hands and dried them on a hot-air drier and found this so funny that we washed them again and dried them a second time. We came out and I followed Baba through the foyer into the lounge. There were a lot of people sitting at the tables, people drinking and talking and flirting with one another. Under the pink, soothing lights all of these people looked smooth and composed, and their faces were not at all like the faces of men who drank in Jack Holland's public house. It would have been nice if we were coming in to drink by ourselves and look at people and admire the jewellery that some of the women wore.

Baba stood on her toes and I saw her wave airily over towards a corner table. I followed her across, a little unsteady on my high heels.

Two middle-aged men stood up and she introduced me. I wasn't sure which was which; but even under such kind lights both were obviously unattractive. They had already had a few drinks and the empty glasses were on the table between them.

'You're at college too, I hear,' the man with the grey hair said to me. The man with the black hair was complimenting Baba on how well she looked so I took it that he was Reginald; and this was Harry who had just spoken to me.

'Yes,' I said. I was sitting on the edge of my chair as if I were waiting for the chandelier over my head to fall on me. It was a nice chandelier, much nicer than the big one over in the centre of the room.

'What's your subject?'

'English,' I said quickly.

'Oh how interesting. I have more than a flair for English myself. As a matter of fact, I have a theory about Shakespeare's sonnets.'

Just then a boy came over to take our order.

'Pink gin,' Baba said, imitating a little girl's voice for Reginald.

'I'll have the same,' I said to the boy. He wiped the glass-topped table clean, and took the empty glasses away. When he came back with the drinks neither of them offered to pay at first and then they both offered the money at the same moment and finally Harry paid and left a two-shilling tip. The pink gin sounded better than it tasted and I asked if I could have a bottle of orange. The orange drowned the bitter taste of the gin.

I didn't want to talk about Shakespeare's sonnets because I only knew one of them by heart, so I said to Reginald, 'Do you work hard?'

'Work! No I'm a confectioner ... I sweeten life. Ha, ha, ha.'

They laughed. I was wondering how many times he had told it before; how worn out it must be by now.

'Laugh, Caithleen, Chrisake laugh,' Baba said and I tried a little laugh, but it didn't work.

Then she said that she wanted to speak to me for a minute and we went out on to the carpeted landing that led to the residents' bathroom.

'Will you do me a favour?' she asked. She was looking up earnestly into my face. I was much taller than her.

'Yes,' I said; and though I was no longer afraid of her I had that sick feeling which I always have before someone says an unpleasant thing to me.

'Will you for Chrisake stop asking fellas if they read James Joyce's, *Dubliners?* They're not interested. They're out for a night. Eat and drink all you can and leave James Joyce to blow his own trumpet.'

'He's dead.'

'Well for God's sake, then, what are you worrying about?'

'I'm not worrying. I just like him.'

'Oh, Caithleen! Why don't you get sense?'

'I hate it. I'll scream if that lump Harry touches me.'

'He won't, Caithleen. We'll all stick together. Think of the dinner. We'll have lamb and mint sauce. Mint sauce, Caithleen, you like it.' She could be very sweet when she wanted to coax me into a good humour. I sent her back to them and I went upstairs and sat in front of a mirror for a while. Just to be away from them.

And I thought of all the people downstairs enjoying themselves and I thought especially of the women, cool and rich and mysterious. It is easy for a woman to be mysterious when she is rich. And for no reason that I could understand, I remembered back to the time when I was four or five and I got a clean nightdress and a clean handkerchief on Saturday nights.

When I came down, they were ready to leave. We were going out to a country hotel for dinner.

Baba sat in the back seat with Reginald. They were giggling and whispering all the time and I was ashamed to look back in case they were embracing or anything like that.

'Well, to go back to this business of Shakespeare's sonnets,' Harry said. He was still droning away when we drove up to the hotel, at the foot of the Sugarloaf mountain. It was a white Georgian house with pine trees all round it. There were masses of daffodils on the front lawn. They were far nicer and far happier than any other daffodils that I had ever seen anywhere else.

'Must get a flower, boys,' Baba said, walking precariously, on her icicle heels, over the marbled chips. 'Boys!' How could she be so false? She was a little drunk. I made an attempt to follow her, because I didn't want to be alone with them, but half-way across I felt that they were measuring me from behind, and I couldn't walk another step. My legs failed me.

'My dish is a lovely dish,' I heard Harry say, and when Baba came back with her button nose in the daffodil cup there were tears in my eyes.

'Jesus, I'll never bring you out again,' she muttered.

'I'll never come,' I said under my breath.

Before dinner we had sherry. The men played darts in the public bar and Harry stood a round of drinks to the local boys. You could see him swell with importance when they raised the glasses of stout and wished 'Happy Easter, sir.'

We had lamb and mint sauce, as Baba promised, and there was a dish of boiled potatoes and some tinned peas. Reginald took three potatoes at once and asked the girl to bring him a double whiskey.

'Eat up, Reg,' Harry said, with contempt in his voice. Harry ordered red wine for us. It was bitter but I forgave its bitterness because of its colour. It was nice just to hold the glass up to the evening light and look through it at the brick fireplace and the copper pans along the wall.

'You're a grand girl,' Harry said.

'I hate you,' I said to myself but aloud I said: 'It's a grand dinner.'

'You're artistic,' he said, touching my glass with his. 'You know a thing about me? I'm artistic too. I had a little hobby once and you know what it was?'

'No.' How the hell could I?

'I made chairs, beautiful Hepplewhite chairs out of match-boxes. Artistic chairs. You'd like them. You're artistic. Let's drink to that,' and they all drank and Reg said, 'Bravo.'

'Happy?' Baba asked me and I cut her with a look.

'You know, I understand you,' Harry said, moving his chair closer to mine. I was uneasy with him. Apart from despising him, I felt he was the kind of man who would get in a huff if you neglected to pass him the peas. I decided to drink, and drink, and drink, until I was very drunk.

'More potatoes, miss?' Reginald asked, as the girl came up the room with a tray of desserts. He had his elbows on the table and was resting his head on his hands. He was asleep when the potatoes came, so she took them away again, and she took his dinner-plate and the bread-plate that was piled high with potato skins.

'Come on now, eat your trifle.' Baba shook him, and his round, small, pig eyes focused on the plate of trifle underneath.

'Sure. Sure.' He ate it quickly as if he couldn't get enough of it. Harry ate with great precision. We had a Gaelic coffee, which was so rich and creamy that I felt sick after it. Then Reginald paid the bill and stuffed a note into the girl's apron pocket.

We drove back just after ten o'clock and there was a stream of cars coming from the opposite direction.

'Sit close to me, will you?' Harry said, in an exasperated way. As if I ought to know the price of a good dinner. Obediently I sat near him. I thought that the worst was over now and that we were going home to our little room.

'Closer,' he said. The way he spoke, you'd think I was a dog.

'Isn't the traffic terrible?' I said. 'You're a great driver,' I added. All I wanted was to get home safely. We were within inches of death three or four times. Reginald began to snore, and Baba put her elbows on the back of my seat and began to talk. She was talking foolishly, about being a virgin, and she was very drunk.

'What's this?' I asked. The car had slowed down outside a large, detached, Tudor-style residence.

'This is home,' Harry said. The double gates were open and he drove the car in within an inch or two of the white garage door. We got out.

There was a cherry tree flowering over near the railings and the lawn was smooth and cared for.

'Don't leave me,' I whispered to Baba as we went up the steps.

'Christ sake, shut up,' she said. She took off her shoes and climbed in her stockinged feet. Reginald picked her up in his arms and carried her into the hallway. Harry switched on the lights and we followed him into the drawing-room. It was a big room with a high ceiling and it was full of expensive furniture. You could smell the money.

We took off our coats and laid them on the sofa. Harry clicked a button and the front of a mahogany cabinet opened out, displaying all sorts of bottles.

'What will it be?' he asked.

'Let's all have "Scotch on the Rocks",' Reginald said, and Baba cooed with furry delight. I said nothing. I had my back to them and was looking at a portrait over the fireplace. It was a woman petting a horse's forehead. His wife I supposed.

'That's my wife,' Harry said as he handed me a huge drink.

'How *is* Betty?' Reginald said. Determined to be bluff about her.

'Fine. She's gone down to the West for a golf championship,' he said, taking off his jacket. He had a fawn buttoned cardigan underneath and he pulled it down over his hips and swaggered in front of me. His body was fat and vain and idiotic.

'Come back, Betty,' I begged the plain horse-faced woman in the oak frame. He drew the curtains. They were the most sumptuous curtains I had ever seen. They were plum velvet and they hung to the floor in soft rich folds. A pelmet of the same material came down in waves over the curtains and they were fringed with red and white tassels. Mama would have loved them.

'Sit down,' he said, and I sank into the high-cushioned

sofa. He sat beside me and began to stroke my hair.

'Happy?' he asked. Reginald and Baba were playing a duet on the piano. The piano-stool was long enough for them to sit side by side.

'I'd love some tea,' I said. Anything to keep us moving.

'Tea?' he repeated, as if it were something that only savages drank.

'Come on, Cait, we'll make tea,' Baba said, getting up off the piano-stool and patting her hair with her hands to keep the waves in place. Harry showed us the kitchen and went back sulkily to drink.

'Christ, can we feck anything?' she said, opening the door of the big white refrigerator. A light came on inside when the door was opened and we looked in eagerly, expecting to see a few cold chickens. The metal racks were perfectly empty: there was nothing but a tray of ice cubes in a metal box.

'Help yourself,' Baba said, standing back so that I could have a full view.

We made the tea and carried the tray back to the drawing-room. There was no milk but the black tea was better than nothing.

'Harry, can I show Barbara your oils?' Reginald said and Harry said 'Certainly.' Reginald took Baba's hand and they went out of the room. I yawned and called after her not to be long.

'At last,' Harry said, laying his drink on the brass table and approaching me with a look of determination. I had my legs crossed and my hands folded demurely on my lap. I looked up at him with a look of nonchalance but underneath I was trembling. He sat on the couch and kissed me fiercely on the lips.

'Come on,' he said, and he tried to lift one knee off the other. The light from behind was shining on his face and his smile was strange.

'No. Let's talk,' I said, trying to be casual.

'I'll tell you a fairy story,' he said.

'Do. Do that. That's nice,' I smiled and accepted another drink. Talk, that was what I must do. Talk. Talk. Talk. And all would be well and I would get home somehow, and make a novena in thanksgiving.

'Ready?' he asked and I nodded and crossed my legs again. He held my hand and I endured it for peace's sake. He began:

'Once upon a time there was a cock and a fox and a pussy cat and they lived on an island far away ...'

It wasn't a long story and though I didn't understand it fully I knew that it was dirty and double-meaning and that he was a dirty, horrible, stupid man.

I stood up and said hysterically, 'I want to go home.'

'Cold little bitch. Cold bitch,' he said, swigging a long drink.

'You're vile and horrible,' I said. I had lost control of my temper.

'And why in God's name did you come, so?' he asked as I went to the door and called Baba. She came downstairs fastening the gold chain round her waist.

'I want to go home,' I said frantically. 'Where's Reginald?'

'He's asleep,' she said. She took her shoes off the ball table and went into the room for our coats.

She asked Harry if he would take us home and he put on his jacket and came out waving a bunch of keys venomously.

It was nice to come out in the air and find the lawn white

with moonlight. The lawn and the moonlight had dignity. Life was beautiful if one only met the beautiful people. Life was beautiful and full of promise. The promise one felt when one looked at a summer garden of hazy blue flowers at the foot of an incredibly beautiful fountain. And in the air were the sprays of hazy silver water that would descend to drench the blue parched flowers.

I sat in the back. He drove quickly and I expected him to kill us.

At the top of our avenue Baba said we'd get out because he might never turn the big car once he came into the narrow avenue.

'Good night, Barbara. You're a nice girl and if I can ever be of help don't forget to give me a ring,' he said to her, and to me he said good night.

We walked quickly up the street. It was chilly and the gardens seemed to be frozen over. It was bright from the moon and the stars and the street lights, and all the curtains were drawn in all the windows. There was a light behind one window and a baby's cry came from that direction.

'Here, Jesus, we might as well have this much,' she said, pulling a guest towel, two tomatoes, and a jar of chicken and ham paste from somewhere inside her dress.

'How in the hell did you get them?'

'When I went out with Reg. He fell asleep so I went rooting round the house; and these condiments were in a press in the kitchen.' She handed me a tomato. I shone it on the sleeve of my coat and bit it. It was sweet and juicy and I was glad of it because I was thirsty after all that drink.

'What happened to you?' she asked.

'What happened to me! That fellow should be shot,' I said.

'Carrying on like a bloody lunatic; why didn't you slap his face?'

'Did *you* slap Reginald?'

'No I didn't. We're going steady. I like him.'

'Is he married?' I asked.

'Could we be going steady if he was married?' she said, sharply.

'He looks married,' I said, but I didn't care. I was happy. It was all over and here we were walking up the pavement under the trees at one o'clock. Tomorrow was Sunday, so I could sleep late. I danced a little, because I was so happy and the tomato was nice and life was just beginning.

There was a small black car parked farther up. It seemed to be outside our gate or the gate next to ours. As we came nearer I saw the window being lowered and when we got up to it I saw that it was him. He smiled, moved over to the window near the kerb and opened the door. I came forward to meet him.

'Oh, Mr Gentleman,' Baba said, surprised.

'Hello,' I said. He looked very tired but he was pleased to see us. You could see by his eyes that he was pleased. They were excited-looking.

'This is a shocking hour of the night to be coming home,' he said. He was looking at me.

'Shocking,' said Baba as she went in the gate. She didn't bother to close it and it gave a clank.

'Leave the key in the door,' I called. I got into the car and we sat near to one another. The gear lever was in the way of our knees so we got out and sat in the back. His face was cold when he kissed me.

'You've been drinking,' he said.

'Yes, I have. I was lonely,' I said.

'Me too. Not drinking but lonely,' and he kissed me again. His lips were cold, beautifully cold like the ice in the cocktail glasses.

'Tell me everything,' he said, but before I could talk or before he could listen we had to embrace each other for a long time. Once during a kiss I opened my eyes to steal a look at his face. The street light was shining directly on the car. His eyes were closed tight, his lashes trembling on his cheeks and his carved, pale face was the face of an old, old man. I closed my own eyes and thought only of his lips and his cold hands and the warm heart that was beating beneath the waistcoat and the starched white shirt. It was then I remembered to take off my coat and show him my blouse. He pushed up the dancing sleeves and kissed my arms from the wrist to the elbow, in a row of light consecutive kisses.

'Will we go somewhere?' he asked.

'Where?'

'Let's drive out and look at the sea.'

We got into the front seat and drove off.

'Are you long there, waiting?' I asked.

'Since midnight. I asked your landlady when you'd be back.'

'You sent me no postcard from Spain,' I said.

'No,' he said, matter-of-factly. 'But I thought of you most of the time.'

He caught my hand. His clasp was at once delicate and savage. Then when he kissed me, my body became like rain. Soft. Flowing. Amenable.

And though it was nice to sit there facing the sea, I thought of us as being somewhere else. In the woods, close together, beside a little stream. A secret place. A green place with ferns all about.

'And you got expelled?' he remarked.

'Yes, we wrote a bad thing,' I said. I blushed, wondering if Martha had told him exactly.

'You funny little girl,' he said and smiled. At first I was indignant at his calling me a funny little girl, and then I found his words sweet. Everything after that was touched with sweetness and enchantment.

That was how I came to see dawn rising over Dublin Bay. It was a cold dawn and the sea desolately grey underneath. We had been sitting there for hours, talking and smoking and embracing. We had admired the green lights across the harbour; we had gazed at each other in the partial darkness and we had said lovely things to one another. Then dawn came, the green lights went out quite suddenly as one white seagull rose into the sky.

'Would you like it if it was moonlight all day long?' I said. 'No. I like the mornings and the daylight.' His voice was dull and sleepy and remote. He was gone from me again.

He backed the car towards the sand-dunes that were half covered with grass and turned it round, quickly and skil-fully. We drove over the smooth sands. The tide was coming in, and I knew that it would wash away the marks of the wheels and I would never be able to come back and find them. We were quiet and strange. It was always like that, with Mr Gentleman. He slipped away, just when things were perfect, as if he couldn't endure perfection.

He left me at my own gate. I wished that I could ask him in for breakfast. But I was afraid of Joanna.

'Are we friends?' I said, anxiously.

'We are,' he said and he smiled at me. We made a date for Wednesday.

'Are you going off home now?' I asked.

'Yes.' He looked sad and cold and I wanted to tell him so.

'Think of me,' he said, as he drove off.

Joanna was cooking sausages when I went in, and she blessed herself when she saw me. I ate my breakfast and went straight to bed. That was the first Sunday I missed Mass.

18

Gradually in the weeks that followed Baba and I became strangers. I went out with Mr Gentleman as often as he was free, and she met Reginald every night. She didn't even come home from class in the evenings and she wore her best coat going out in the morning.

'Go to rot,' Joanna said at the breakfast table when she saw our faces pale for want of sleep and our fingers brown from nicotine.

'Go to hell,' Baba said. Her cough was getting worse and she had got thinner.

Three days later she told me that she had to go to a sanatorium for six months. Reginald had made her have an X-ray and it was found that she had tuberculosis.

'Oh, Baba,' I said, going round to her side of the table to put my arms round her. Why had we become strangers? Why were we sharp and secretive in the last few weeks? I put my cheek close to hers.

'Christ, don't, there's probably germs floating every-where around me,' she said and I laughed. Her face was pale now, and the boyish bloom was going off it. She looked older and wiser in the last few weeks. Was it Reginald? Or was it her sickness? She got her case ready.

'I'm leaving some clothes here and don't you be sporting

them every damn' day,' she said as she put two summer dresses back on a hanger.

Later on Reginald's car hooted outside the gate and I called up to ask her if she was ready.

I helped her into her tweed coat in the hallway. The lining of one sleeve was all ripped but finally we got her arm in. She stood for a minute, very small and thin with a deep flush in both cheeks. Her blue eyes were misted over with the beginnings of tears and she bit at her bottom lip to try and stop herself from crying. Then she put on some pinkish lipstick and smiled at herself bravely in the hall mirror.

Joanna took off her apron in case Reginald should come in.

'I'll visit you as often as I can,' I said to Baba. She was going to a sanatorium in Wicklow and I knew that I couldn't afford the bus fare more than once a week. Mr Brennan was to pay £3 a week for her there.

'Smoke like hell when you come, so's you won't get any goddam' bugs around the place,' she said. She was still smiling.

Gustav and Joanna said good-bye to her and Reginald brought out the case and put a rug round her when she got into the car. He was very attentive to her and I was beginning to like him.

I waved to the car and she waved back. Her thin white fingers behind the glass waved to the end of our friendship. She was gone. It would never be the same again, not even if we tried.

Joanna went upstairs to spray disinfectant all over the room, and she grumbled about having to wash the blankets again, when they were washed only a few months before.

The way she grumbled you'd think Baba went and got the tuberculosis on purpose.

The bedroom was tidy but deserted. Baba's make-up and the huge flagon of perfume Reginald gave her, these were gone and the dressing-table was bare. She left the blue necklace on my bed with a note. It said: *To Caithleen in remembrance of all the good times we had together. You're a right-looking eejit.* It was then I cried for her, and thought of all the evenings we walked home from school and how she used to set dogs after me, and write dirty words on my arm with indelible pencil.

I was fidgety and I bit my nails because I had to ask Joanna a favour.

'Joanna, can I have a friend in the drawing-room tonight?'

'Mine Got, you give the house a bad name. The ladies next door, they say, "What kind of girls you got, keeping disgrace hours?"'

'He's rich,' I said. I knew this would impress her. Joanna had some notion that if a rich man came into the house, he'd leave five-pound notes under the tablecloth, or forget his overcoat on purpose and leave it behind for Gustav. She was simple that way. I could see the look of hope that came into her stupid blue eyes when I said that he was rich. Finally she said yes, and I began to get ready for my date.

It is the only time that I am thankful for being a woman, that time of evening, when I draw the curtains, take off my old clothes and prepare to go out. Minute by minute the excitement grows. I brush my hair under the light and the colours are autumn leaves in the sun. I shadow my eyelids with black stuff and am astonished by the look of mystery it gives to my eyes. I hate being a woman. Vain and shallow and superficial. Tell a woman that you love her and she'll ask you to write it down, so that she can show it to her friends. But I am happy at that time of night. I feel tender towards the world, I pet the wallpaper as if it were white rose petals flushed pink at the edges; I pick up my old, tired shoes and they are silver flowers that some man has laid outside my door. I kissed myself in the mirror and ran out of the room, happy and hurried and suitably mad.

I was late and Mr Gentleman was annoyed. He handed me an orchid that was two shades of purple – pale purple and dark. I pinned it to my cardigan.

We went to a restaurant off Grafton Street, and climbed the narrow stairs to a dark, almost dingy, little room. It had red and white striped wallpaper, and there was a black-brown portrait over the fireplace. It was in a thick gilt frame and I wasn't sure whether it was a portrait of a man or a woman, because the hair was covered with a black mop cap. We sat over near the window. It was half open, the nylon curtains blew inwards and brushed the tablecloth lightly and fanned our faces. As usual we were very shy. The curtains were white and foamy like summer clouds and he was wearing a new paisley tie.

'Your tie is nice,' I said stiffly.

'You like it?' he asked. It was agony until the first drink came and then he melted a little and smiled at me. Then the room seemed charming, with its lighted red candle in a wine bottle on the table. I shall never forget the pallor of his high cheek-bones when he bent down to pick up his napkin. He patted my knee for a second and then looked at me with one of his slow, intense, tormented looks.

'I feel hungry,' he said.

'I feel hungry,' I said. Little did he know that I ate two shop buns on my way to meet him. I loved shop buns, especially iced ones.

'For all sorts of things,' he said, as he scooped some melon with a spoon. He reminded me of the melon. Cool and cold and bloodless and refreshing. He twined his ankles round mine under the big linen tablecloth and the evening began to be perfect. Candle-grease dripped on to the cloth.

We drove home after eleven and he was pleased when I asked him in. I was ashamed of the hallway and the cheap carpet on the stairs. There was a stale, musty smell in the drawing-room when we went in first. He sat down on the sofa and I sat on a high-backed chair across the table from him. I was happy from the wine and I told him about my life and how I fell in the dance hall and went upstairs to drink minerals for the rest of the night. He was amused, but he didn't laugh outright. Always the remote, enchanting smile. I had drunk a lot and I was giddy. But the tiny remaining sober part of me watched the rest of me being happy and listened to the happy, foolish things that I said.

'Come over near me,' he asked and I came and sat very quietly beside him. I could feel him trembling.

'You're happy?' he said, tracing the outline of my face with his finger.

'Yes.'

'You're going to be happier.'

'How?'

'We're going to be together. I'm going to make love to you.' He spoke in a half whisper and kept looking, uneasily, towards the window, as if there might be someone watching us from the back garden. I went over and drew the blind, as there were no curtains in that room. I was blushing when I came back to sit down.

'Do you mind?' he asked.

'When? Now?' I clutched the front of my cardigan, and looked at him earnestly. He said that I looked appalled. I wasn't appalled really. Just nervous, and sad in some way, because the end of my girlhood was near.

'Sweetling,' he said. He put an arm round me and brought my head down on his shoulder, so that my cheek touched his neck. Some tears of mine must have trickled down inside his collar. He patted my knees with his other band. I was excited, and warm, and violent.

'Do you know French?' he asked.

'No. I did Latin at school,' I said. Imagine talking about school at a time like that. I could have killed myself for being so juvenile.

'Well, there's a French word for it. It means ... a ... atmosphere. We'll go away to the right atmosphere for a few weeks.'

'Where?' I thought with horror of bacon-and-egg hotels across the central towns of Ireland with ketchup dribbles on the relish bottles and gravy stains on the check cloth. And rain outside. But I might have known that he would be more careful. He always was. Even to the extent of parking his car right outside the restaurants where we ate, so that no one would see us walking up the street to the car park.

'To Vienna,' he said and my heart did a few somersaults.

'Is it nice there?'

'It's very nice there.'

'And what will we do?'

'We'll eat and go for walks. And in the evenings we'll go up to eating places in the mountains and sit there drinking wine and looking down at the town. And then we'll go to bed.' He said it quite simply and I loved him more than I would ever love a man again.

'Is it good to go?' I asked. I just wanted him to reassure me.

'Yes. It's good. We have to get this out of our systems.' He frowned a little; and I had a vision of coming back to the same room and the same life and being without him.

'But I want you for always,' I said, imploringly. He smiled and kissed me lightly on the cheeks. Kisses like the first drops of rain. 'You'll always love me?' I asked.

'You know I don't like you to talk like that,' he said, playing with the top button of my cardigan.

'I know,' I said.

'Then why do you?' he asked, tenderly.

'Because I can't help it. Because I'd go mad if I hadn't you.'

He looked at me for a long time. That look of his which was half sexual, half mystic; and then he said my name very gently. ('Caithleen.') I could hear the bulrushes sighing when he said my name that way and I could hear the curlew too and all the lonesome sounds of Ireland.

'Caithleen. I want to whisper you something.'

'Whisper,' I said. I put my hair behind my ear and he held it there because it had a habit of falling back into its old place. He leaned over and put his mouth close to my ear and kissed it first and said, 'Show me your body. I've never seen your legs or breasts or anything. I'd like to see you.'

'And if I'm not nice then will you change your mind?' I had inherited my mother's suspiciousness.

'Don't be silly,' he said and he helped me take off my cardigan. I was trying to decide whether to take off my blouse or my skirt first.

'Don't look,' I said. It was difficult. I didn't like him to see suspenders and things. I peeled off my skirt and everything under it, and then my blouse and my cotton vest, and finally I unclasped my brassière, the black one; and I stood there shivering a little, not knowing what to do with my arms. So I put my hand up to my throat, a gesture that I often do when I am at a loss. The only place I felt warm was where my hair covered my neck and the top part of my back. I came over and sat beside him and nestled in near him for a little warmth.

'You can look now,' I said and he took his hand down from his eyes and looked shyly at my stomach and my thighs.

'Your skin is whiter than your face. I thought it would be pink,' he said and he kissed me all over.

'Now we won't be shy when we get there. We've seen one another,' he said.

'I haven't seen you.'

'Do you want to?' and I nodded. He opened his braces and let his trousers slip down around his ankles. He took off his other things and sat down quickly. He was not half so distinguished out of his coal-black suit and stiff white shirt. Something stirred in the garden or was it in the hall? I thought what horror if Joanna should burst in in her nightdress and find us like two naked fools on the green velveteen couch. And she would shout for Gustav, and the ladies next door would hear her and the police would come.

I looked down slyly at his body and laughed a little. It was so ridiculous.

'What's so funny?' He was piqued that I should laugh.

'It's the colour of the pale part of my orchid,' I said and I looked over at my orchid that was still pinned to my cardigan. I touched it. Not my orchid. His. It was soft and incredibly tender, like the inside of a flower, and it stirred. It reminded me when it stirred of a little black man on top of a collecting box that shook his head every time you put a coin in the box. I told him this and he kissed me fiercely and for a long time.

'You're a bad girl,' he said.

'I like being a bad girl,' I replied, wide-eyed.

'No, not really, darling. You're sweet. The sweetest girl I ever met. My country girl with country-coloured hair,' and he buried his face in it and smelt it for a minute.

'Darling, I'm not made of iron,' he said and he stood up and drew his trousers up from around his ankles. When I got up to fetch my clothes he fondled my bottom and I knew that our week together would be beautiful.

'I'll make you a cup of tea,' I said after we had dressed ourselves and he had combed his hair with my comb.

We went out to the kitchen on tip-toe. I lit the gas and filled the kettle noiselessly by letting the water from the tap pour down the side of the kettle. The refrigerator was locked because of Herman's fits of night hunger, but I found a few old biscuits in a forgotten tin. They were soft but he ate them. After the tea he left. It was Friday so he was making the long journey down the country. On week nights he stayed in a men's club in Stephen's Green.

I stood at the door and he let down the window of the car and waved good night. He drove away without making any noise at all. I came in, put my orchid in a cup of water, and carried it upstairs to the orange box beside my bed. I was too happy to go to sleep.

19

Some men came and lopped the trees that skirted the pavement. They left nothing but the short fat branches that somehow looked obscene. The feathery branches were gone and the buds too. It was the wrong time of year to lop trees and I could never understand why they did it then, unless that people had complained about the light being shut out from their sitting-rooms.

But I was so happy I hardly noticed the trees. We were going away together. He was going on one aeroplane to London and I was following on the next one. He said it was better that way, in case we should be seen at the airport.

I was so happy and he was happy too. Sitting in the drawing-room for hours I used to look at his face, his bony ascetic face with his fine nose and his eyes that were always saying things, eyes that flashed amber because of the yellow lampshade on the table-light. Some nights I put on the electric heater and I was afraid Joanna would smell it upstairs.

'You know what worries me?' he said, catching my hands and stroking them.

'Your low blood pressure; or maybe your age?' I said, smiling.

'No,' and he gave me a gentle slap on the face.

'What then?'

'The coming back. Being separated.'

But I didn't think about that. I only thought of going.

'Did you ever go before?' I asked, nervously.

'Don't ask me that.' He was frowning a little. His forehead was yellow-white, as if he had lemon juice, instead of blood, under his skin.

'Why not?'

'It's pointless, really. If I say "yes", it will only make you sad.'

And already I was sad. No one would ever really belong to him. He was too detached.

'I'll watch you as you come down the aeroplane runway,' he said. Then he got out his diary and we tried to fix a date. I had to go out of the room to think; not every week suited me, and I couldn't think when his arms were round me. Finally we settled a week, and he made a note of it in pencil.

In the days that followed I thought only of it. When I was washing my neck, I made a soap lather for him, and when I was weighing sugar in the shop, I was singing to myself. I gave children free sugar barleys and I bought Willie a dickie bow for his Sunday shirt. Going along the street I talked to myself all the time. Arranging conversations between us, smiling at everyone; helping old women to cross the road and flirting with bus conductors.

A few little things worried me. I had to ask for the week off. Mr Burns was easy to handle, but sleepy-eyed Mrs Burns could read your mind.

Also I had stopped going to Mass and Confession and things. But most of all, I hadn't enough underwear. I wanted a blue flowing transparent nightgown. So that we could waltz before we got into bed. To tell you the truth, I always shirked a little at the actual getting into bed.

Mama had nice nightdresses but I left them in the drawers, and I didn't know if my father got them before the furniture was auctioned. I could have written to ask him, but at the thought of him my heart started to race. I hadn't written for six weeks and I didn't want to write any more. Mr Gentleman mentioned that my father had flu, and that the nuns were looking after him.

Then I thought of asking Joanna. Joanna and I had got very friendly since Baba went away. I helped with the washing-up and we went to the pictures, one night after tea. Joanna laughed so much that she was snorting in the back of her nose and the couple near us were horrified.

'I'm going to Vienna,' I said, as we walked home through the fresh spring night. There was a smell of night-scented stock. She linked me and I was uncomfortable about this. I hate women linking me.

'Mine Got! For what?'

'With a friend,' I said, carelessly.

'A man?' she asked, opening her eyes very wide and looking with astonishment as if men were monsters.

'Yes,' I said. It was easy talking to Joanna.

'The rich man?' she asked.

'The rich man,' I added; and a sudden anxiety came to me about paying my fare and my hotel bill. Did he expect me to pay my own?

'Good. It is beautiful there. The opera, lovely. I remember my brothers spending me a night at the opera for my twenty-one birthday. They gave me a wrist-watch. Fifteen-carat gold.' It was the nearest Joanna ever got to being nostalgic. I was still worrying about the money for the aeroplane ticket.

'Will you loan me a nightdress?' I asked.

She said nothing for a moment and then she said: 'Yes. But you must be very careful. It is from my own honeymoon. Thirty years old.' I blanched a little and held the gate open for her. Gustav was at the door with his hands stretched out, like a man begging for alms. There was something wrong.

'Herman. He do it again, Joanna,' he said. Joanna shot in the door and rushed up the stairs. She took two steps at a time and you could see the legs of her knickers. A torrent of German ascended ahead of her. I heard her rattle the door-knob of Herman's room, and then knock on the door and pound it and call, 'Herman, Herman, you leave this night,' and Herman said nothing. But when I went up there seemed to be crying from behind his door. He had been in bed all day with flu.

'What's wrong?' I thought they were all mad.

'His kidneys. He has kidney trouble. The best hair mattress and my good pure linen sheets,' Joanna said. We stood in the narrow landing waiting for him to open his door and Joanna began to cry.

'Leave him, Joanna, until morning.' Gustav came up and stood on the step where the stairs turned left. She cried more and talked about the mattress and the sheets and you could see that Gustav was embarrassed because of her. She took off her white knitted coat and picked loose hairs off the collar.

I went into my own room and in a few minutes she came in after me. She had the nightdress in her hand. It was folded in tissue paper and, as she opened the paper, camphor balls kept falling out and rolling on to the floor. It was lilac colour and it was the biggest nightdress I'd ever seen. I put it on and looked like a girl playing Lady Macbeth for the Sacred Heart Players. I was shapeless in it. I tied the purple sash tight round the waist, but it was still hickish.

'Lovely. Pure silk,' she said, fingering the deep frill that fell over my hand and almost covered it.

'Lovely,' I agreed. He would smell the camphor and sneeze for the entire week and go home trying to remember which of his grand-aunts I resembled. Still it was better than nothing.

'Show Gustav,' she said, arranging it so that it fell in loose pleats from around the waist. She held it up while I went down the stairs as if I were wearing a wedding dress.

Gustav got red and said, 'Very smart.'

'You remember, Gustav?' she said. She was grinning at him.

'No, Joanna.' He was reading the advertisements in the evening paper. He said that Herman would have to go and they would get a nice proper gentleman.

'You remember, Gustav?' she said, going over to him. But Gustav said 'No' as if he wanted to forget. Joanna was hurt.

'They are all the same,' she said, as we prepared the tray for supper. 'All men they are all the same. No soft in them,' and I thought of something very soft about my Mr Gentleman. Not his face. Not his nature. But a part of his soft, beseeching body.

'Mind you not fill up with baby,' she said. I laughed. It was impossible. I had an idea that couples had to be married for a long time before a woman got a baby.

I kept the nightdress on during supper because I had my other clothes under it. We sat very late looking through all the advertisements, and finally Gustav found one that was suitable.

'Italian musician requires full board in foreign household,' and he got the ink off the sideboard and Joanna spread a newspaper over the velvet cloth, then unlocked the china cabinet and took out a sheet of headed paper. It was locked because Herman was in the habit of stealing sheets of it to write to his mother and his sisters.

There was a skin on my cocoa and I lifted it off with my spoon. The cocoa was cold.

Gustav put on his glasses and Joanna got him the old fountain-pen that had no top on it. One they found out on the road. It wrote like a post-office pen.

'What date is it, Joanna?' he asked. She went over to the calendar on the wall and looked at it, screwing up her eyes.

'May 15th,' she said and I felt myself go cold. The morning paper was on the tea trolley and I reached over the back of my armchair and picked it up. There on the very first page under the anniversaries was a memorium for my mother. Four years. Four short years and I had forgotten the date of her death; at least I had overlooked it! I felt that wherever she was she had stopped loving me, and I went out of the room crying. It was worse to think that he had remembered. I recalled it in my head, the short, simple insertion, signed with my father's name.

'Caithleen.' Joanna followed me out to the hall.

'It's nothing,' I said over the banisters. 'It's nothing, Joanna.'

But all that night I slept badly. I tucked my legs up under my nightdress and I was shivering. I was waiting for someone to come and warm me. I think I was waiting for Mama. And all the things I am afraid of kept coming into my mind. Drunk men. Shouting. Blood. Cats. Razor blades. Galloping horses. The night was terrifying and the bathroom door kept slamming. I got up to close it around three and filled myself a hot-water bottle from the hot tap. It wasn't my own and I knew that if Baba were there now she'd warn me that it would give me some damn' disease like athlete's foot or eczema or something. I missed Baba. She kept me sane. She kept me from brooding about things.

I came back to bed and Joanna wakened me with a cup of tea just after eight o'clock. When I opened my eyes she was drawing back the curtains to let the sun in. I looked up at the cracked grey ceiling and wasn't afraid any more. We were going away the following Saturday.

I drank the tea, fondled my stomach for a while, and soon as I heard Herman move next door I jumped out, so as to have the first of the bathroom.

20

The next week flew. I plucked my eyebrows, packed my case, and bought postcards, so that I could send some to Joanna. I was afraid that I mightn't get to buy any there. I washed my hair-brush and put it out on the window-sill to dry and borrowed two of Baba's dresses. Writing to Baba, I told her I had flu, but said nothing about borrowing the dresses, nor about going away. You couldn't trust Baba.

On Thursday morning there was a letter from Hickey which had been re-addressed from the Brennans'. He said that he was arriving in Dublin on the mail boat the following Tuesday and asked me to meet him. He didn't say whether he was married or not and I was curious to know. His spelling had improved. Of course I had to send him a tele-gram to say I couldn't manage it. Doing this, the thought came to me that I was foolish and disloyal, not only to Hickey, who had been my best friend, but to Jack Holland and Martha and Mr Brennan. To all the real people in my life. Mr Gentleman was but a shadow and yet it was this shadow I craved. I sent the telegram, instantly made myself forget about Hickey, and thought of our holiday in Vienna.

I could see myself sitting up in bed with a big breakfast tray across my lap. I could see the tray and the cups and a brown earthenware dish that was warmed. I would lift the lid off the dish and find fingers of golden toast that the butter had soaked right into. Sometimes in my fantasy he was asleep and I was wakening him by tickling his forehead; and then at other times he was awake and drinking a glass of orange juice. I thought Saturday would never come.

It came and it was raining. The rain upset my plans. I was to wear a white feather hat and I could not possibly let it get wet. It was a lovely hat that fitted tight to the head, and the feathers curved down over my ears and gave my face a soft, feathered look.

When I was leaving the shop at four Mr Burns gave me my wages and a pound extra for the journey home. I told them there was an aunt dying.

'Good God, you can't go out in that rain,' he said.

'I'll miss my train if I don't.' So he went into the hallway and found me an old umbrella. A godsend. I could wear my hat now. I almost kissed him. I think he expected me to, because he smoothed the brown hairs of his moustache.

''Bye, miss,' Willie said, as he held the door for me. It was lashing rain outside. It pelted against my legs and my stockings got drenched. Joanna had tea ready, and she loaned me a little phrase-book that had English and German words in it.

'Mind you not lose,' she warned me. I put it in my handbag.

'I not charge, while you're away,' she said, beaming at me. Everything was working out marvellously. The new lodger was coming that evening so Joanna was happy.

'Mine Got, you are so lovely,' she said, when I came downstairs in my black coat and my white feather hat.

I had made my face pale with pancake make-up and darkened my eyelids with green mascara.

The long coils of auburn hair fell loosely around my shoulders, and though I was tall and well developed around the bust, I had the innocent look of a very young girl. No one would have suspected that I was going off with a man.

I had put my gloves in my bag, so that they wouldn't get wet. They were white kid gloves of Mama's. There were stains of iron mould where they buttoned at the wrist but otherwise they were lovely.

It was still raining when I came out. It was awkward trying to manage the case and the umbrella as well as carry my handbag. A telegram boy went by on a motorcycle and spattered my stockings, so I swore after him. I got a bus immediately and was there twenty minutes too early.

We were meeting outside an amusement palace on the quays. It was convenient for him to pick me up there, as he came up from his office; and neither of us had thought of the rain when we fixed the place.

I stood in the porchway that led to the sweet shop and put my case down. My hands were wet so I wiped them on the lining of my coat. In at the back of the shop there were slot machines and a room where boys played snooker. They were all dressed alike, in coloured jerseys and tight-fitting tartan trousers. They all needed haircuts.

The rain had got less. It was only spotting now. I looked at my watch, his little moth-gold watch; he was ten minutes late. The church bells from the opposite side of the Liffey chimed seven. I looked at all the cars as they came up the quays.

At half-seven I began to get anxious, because I knew that his plane went at half-eight and mine left shortly before nine o'clock. I sat on the edge of my suitcase and tried to look absorbed as the long-haired boys went in and out to play snooker. They were passing remarks about me. I began to count the flagstones on the laneway nearby. I thought, 'He'll come now, while I'm counting, and I won't see the car drive up to the kerb and he'll have to blow the hooter to call me.' I knew the sound of the hooter. But I counted the flagstones three times and he hadn't come. It was nearing eight and there were pigeons and sea-gulls walking along the limestone wall that skirted the river Liffey.

'Are you waiting for someone?' the woman from the sweetshop called out to me. She was fat and her hair was dyed blonde.

'I'm waiting for my father,' I said. 'We're going away somewhere.'

'Come in and sit down,' she said. I went in and sat on a wicker chair. It squeaked when you sat on it. I bought a bottle of orange, just to pass the time, and drank it through a straw. Every few minutes I came out to look. I was getting anxious now, and when he came I'd tell him how anxious and frightened I'd been. I went across the road to look at a Guinness barge that was going up the river. The river was brown and filthy and the top of the wall was spattered white from all the bird droppings. His small black car came buzzing up the quay and I ran to the edge of the footpath and waved. But the car went by. It was exactly like his, except that the registration number was not the same. I went back to finish my orange.

'Kill you, wouldn't it,' the blonde woman said to me. Her name was Dolly. The boys playing snooker called her that and were fresh with her.

My whole body was impatient now. I couldn't sit still. My body was wild from waiting. The street lights came on outside, the wet bulbs gave out a blurred yellow light, and the street took on that look of night mystery that I always love. The raindrops hung to the iron bars that held up the grey awning, they clung to it for a while and then they dropped on to a man's hat as he went by. I think it was then that I admitted to myself for the first time that he just might not be coming. But only for the shadow of a second did I allow myself to think of it. I bought a woman's magazine and looked for my horoscope. The magazine was a week old so my horoscope was of no help.

'Afraid, love, we're closing up now,' Dolly said. 'Wouldju like to come in and sit in the kitchen for a while?'

I thanked her but said I'd rather not. He might come unknown to me. She took the money out of the cash register, counted it, and put it into a big black purse.

'Good night, love,' she said as she closed the door after me. I sat in the porch. People passed by, with heads lowered. Grey, sad, indiscriminate people, going nowhere. Two sailors passed and winked at me. They kept looking back, but when they saw that I wasn't interested they walked on.

It rained on and off.

I knew now that he wasn't coming; but still I sat there. An hour or two later I got up, picked up my things, and walked despondently towards the bus stop in O'Connell Street.

Joanna rushed out when she heard the gate squeak. Her hands were raised; her fat, greasy face was beaming. The lodger had arrived.

'A real gentleman. Rich. Expensive. You like him, he is so nice. Real pigskin gloves. Goot suit, everything,' she said.

'Come, you meet him,' she caught hold of my wet wrist and tried to coax me. Then she saw that I was crying.

'Oh, a telegram. One came. You had just gone but I could

not follow now because my new man was coming and I could not go out of the house, for fear of he arriving and find nobody.' She was hoping that I wasn't cross. I took off my hat and threw it on the hall-stand. It was a wet, grey hen by now.

'I am sad for you. It is all for best,' Joanna said, as she nodded towards the room.

I opened the telegram. It said:

Everything gone wrong. Threats from your father. My wife has another nervous breakdown. Regret enforced silence. Must not see you.

It was not signed and it had been handed in at a Limerick post office early that morning.

'Come, meet my nice new friend,' Joanna pleaded, but I shook my head and went upstairs to cry.

I cried on the bed for a long time, until I began to feel very cold. Somehow one feels colder, after hours of crying. Eventually I got up and put on the light. I came downstairs to make a cup of tea. The telegram was still in my hand, crumpled into a ball. I read it again. It said exactly the same thing.

After I'd put the kettle on the gas, I went automatically to get my cup off the dining-room table, as Joanna always laid the breakfast things before going to bed. As I came to the door, I heard a sound from within. I peeped round the side of the door and looked straight into the face of a strange young man, who was holding a brass instrument in one hand and a polishing rag in the other.

'I'm sorry,' I said, picked my cup off the table, and ran straight out of the room. My face must have been a nice sight. Blotchy from crying.

When I had made the tea, I recollected that he must think it a very odd house, so I went down the hall and called in, 'Would you like a cup of tea?' I didn't want him to see my face again.

'No English speak,' he said.

'God,' I thought, 'as if it makes any difference to whether you'd like tea or not.'

I poured him a cup and brought it in.

'No English speak,' he said, and he shrugged his shoulders.

I came out to the kitchen and took two aspirins with my tea. It was almost certain that I wouldn't sleep that night.

available from
THE ORION PUBLISHING GROUP

☐ **A Fanatic Heart** £7.99
EDNA O'BRIEN
978–0–7538–1308–9

☐ **House of Splendid Isolation**
£7.99
EDNA O'BRIEN
978–1–8579–9209–0

☐ **Down by the River** £6.99
EDNA O'BRIEN
978–1–8579–9873–3

☐ **James Joyce** £7.99
EDNA O'BRIEN
978–0–7538–1070–5

☐ **Byron in Love** £7.99
EDNA O'BRIEN
978–0–7538–2646–1

☐ **Wild Decembers** £7.99
EDNA O'BRIEN
978–0–7538–0990–7

☐ **In the Forest** £7.99
EDNA O'BRIEN
978–0–7538–1685–1

☐ **The Country Girls** £7.99
EDNA O'BRIEN
978–0–7528–8116–4

☐ **Girls in their Married Bliss**
£6.99
EDNA O'BRIEN
978–0–7538–2138–1

☐ **Girl with Green Eyes** £6.99
EDNA O'BRIEN
978–0–7538–2137–4

All Orion/Phoenix titles are available at your local bookshop or from the following address:

Mail Order Department
Littlehampton Book Services
FREEPOST BR535
Worthing, West Sussex, BN13 3BR
telephone 01903 828503, *facsimile* 01903 828802
e-mail MailOrders@lbsltd.co.uk
(Please ensure that you include full postal address details)

Payment can be made either by credit/debit card (Visa, Mastercard, Access and Switch accepted) or by sending a £ Sterling cheque or postal order made payable to *Littlehampton Book Services*.
DO NOT SEND CASH OR CURRENCY.

Please add the following to cover postage and packing

UK and BFPO:
£1.50 for the first book, and 50p for each additional book to a maximum of £3.50

Overseas and Eire:
£2.50 for the first book plus £1.00 for the second book and 50p for each additional book ordered

----

BLOCK CAPITALS PLEASE

name of cardholder ....

address of cardholder ....

delivery address
(if different from cardholder)

....

....

....

....

....

postcode ....

postcode ....

☐ I enclose my remittance for £.............................

☐ please debit my Mastercard/Visa/Access/Switch (delete as appropriate)

card number ☐☐☐☐☐☐☐☐☐☐☐☐☐☐☐☐☐

expiry date ☐☐☐☐   Switch issue no. ☐☐

signature ....

prices and availability are subject to change without notice